Praise for Gary J. Shipley & *Terminal Park*

"Shipley's *Terminal Park* pounds fiction into entirely new shapes. Disintegrating and blissful. Highly Recommend."
—Tony Burgess, author of *Pontypool Changes Everything*

"Gary J. Shipley's writing has a way of making every form he works within advance, in an overarching sense, such that the next exciting thing you read, no matter how advanced, is rendered a jalopy."
—Dennis Cooper, author of *The Marbled Swarm*

"The world is a void and there are no more prophets left to serve. There is still vision, however, and Shipley's is one we might all surrender to."
—Travis Jeppesen, author of *The Suiciders*

"Shipley's writing is important because it's a fearless attempt to advance the art of literature, to force us to breathe something, to drown in something, to bloody our hands. It's an unforgettable experience."
—3:AM Magazine

TERMINAL PARK

TERMINAL PARK

GARY J. SHIPLEY

Terminal Park

ISBN-13: 978-1-7335694-3-9
ISBN-10: 1-7335694-3-X

Cover design by Gary J. Shipley

www.apocalypse-party.com

Printed in the U.S.A

The great, lethal epidemics have disappeared. They have all been replaced by a single one: the proliferation of human beings themselves. Overpopulation constitutes a kind of slow and irresistible epidemic, the opposite of plague and cholera. We can only hope that it will bring itself to an end once it has been sated with the living as the plague did when sated with dead. Will the same regulatory reflex operate against this excess of life as once did against the excess of death? Because the excess of life is even more lethal.

~ Jean Baudrillard, *Cool Memories*

But what is primal repression? Let us call it the ability of the speaking being, always already haunted by the Other, to divide, reject, repeat.

~ Julia Kristeva, *Powers of Horror*

Who can say in the history of this planet that they've sat in a sun-lounger, 1,450 ft. up, swigging from a ₹20,000 bottle of Cognac as they watch the Arabian Sea turn slowly pink with blood?

The sky over Death Valley was spotted with Lockheed C-5 Galaxies, thousands of human beings sluicing from their back ends like screaming water. Over Siberia, Antonov An-225 Mriyas unfurled their insides into the frozen air, laying pathways of bodies on the permafrost in patterns that served no other purpose than to distract the pilots from the two thousand people they'd just murdered, the ten thousand they'd murdered that day, and the twelve to fifteen thousand they would murder tomorrow, and the day after that, and would continue to murder all the while the fuel lasted out and there were humans to remove.

The Arctic, the Antarctic, (spilling into the Northern and Southern Temperate Zones), Australia, New Zealand, Africa (north and south), the Antarctic and Arctic deserts, the Sahara, the Kalahari, the Great Victorian, the Gobi, Arabian, Patagonian, Syrian, and the Great Basin are all marked out as suitable dumping grounds. But however vast their accumulated area, it would not be enough.

At around five quadrillion the crust of the earth has its own human skin. At ten quadrillion it would be two deep. At fifty quadrillion it would be ten deep. After that, he would begin to calculate how much longer his scraper could hold.

Situated in Lower Parel, South Mumbai and standing at 1450 feet, with 117 floors, the World One Tower was the planet's tallest residential skyscraper, at the topmost point of which he sat and waited and watched as the population continued to swell, the earth beneath it dying, and at the centre of it all the realization that his own thoughts were coming to an end.

It turned out death and meaninglessness were not types of void. They were not deficiencies but excesses. The void is not nothing, the void is too much.

It being virtually impossible to differentiate

between those who'd existed before the population started accelerating and those who had arrived as a result of it, the destruction of other humans soon became indiscriminate. Humanity's greatest achievements, its sciences its arts its literatures its technologies its moral codes, all met in a single plateaued line, in the warm engine of death. All science became the science of more effective murder, all literature the sacrificial soundbites used to induce the reluctant homicide, all art the coagulation of bodies in ever-increasing numbers, all technology weaponization, and all morality the expediential proliferation of human death. The apocalypse was the shark they were swimming towards – and climbing inside, to save themselves.

The line between combatant and civilian was not merely spongiform, it was not even a line. In this war, there were no civilians, no innocents, no crimes against humanity, no collateral damage, no cost of war that wasn't just the cost of existence itself. In the end, the only deviant behavior was paralysis.

The schizophrenic conditioning of war was no longer required, and would of course have been an unnecessary indulgence in a conflict with all the pervasiveness of oxygen, a war without fronts, without armies; a paradoxical war, and the only authentic world war possible: that of mankind against itself and for itself. What had been the epitome of inhumanity fast became its opposite. For those that did not kill were not only failing themselves but all humankind, whose sole hope for survival rested with the swift and extensive depletion of its expanded mass.

Defilers of bodies were no longer Wittkopian rarities, those warped aesthetes of desire, so meticulous, so bent up inside their own weirdness, but were instead your archetypal bros piping their inconsequential vigour into the waning warmth of the dead. Various grunt-ideologies surfaced at the beginning and fast became preconditions for any kind of survival, cultivating previously untapped resources of brutality and ruthlessness with a militarized rhetoric equating the humanistic with the pitiless. But regardless of the success of killing sprees, the achieved corpses were still your enemies, still a contagion to be desecrated in irreligious petrol fires, or fed to pigs or gators or dogs or carnivorous fish. That this moral inversion should be adopted so readily, that atrocity should become the bastion of all human hope, would have surprised even the most intransigent of our moral relativists.

The proclivity for murder permeated privilege and underclass alike. If in the beginning there'd been squeamishness about the universality of noble extermination it corrected itself with an alacrity that the formerly peaceful would have countenanced with a despair that'd rot the senses to a mush. But when all hope for peace was premised on the massacre of billions, no further argument was needed. It moves, you kill it! (in the name of God, Allah, Krishna, decency, whatever the fuck you like): *Caedite eos. Novit enim Dominus qui sunt eius.*

At 4.25 a.m. a fuel-air bomb exploded

in the centre of Tokyo. Every window for a radius of half a mile shattered, buildings at close range razed. 263 people were killed instantly, and over a hundred more were wounded. Around 4.50 a.m., a man in a police uniform arrived at the blast site. Hundreds of people were gathered in and around the carnage, helping the wounded, weeping over the dead. The man pulled an assault rifle from his bag and began shooting indiscriminately, firing in every direction. He killed dozens, chasing his victims into the doorways of half-collapsed buildings, their blown-out windows still belching smoke and flames. Minutes later the police had the man surrounded. At which point a second man, identical to the first, started opening fire on the officers, killing them all. The two men escaped the scene unharmed. Their name is Andrew Singer. They sought global fame online, bragging their crime and further crimes to come. They published a rambling manifesto entitled: "For those of us unborn: duplication and murder in the age of revelation." On their shared blog, each had diagnosed the other as suffering from alexithymia, going on to explain how this had influenced their own behaviour since the fissioning event. In less than one hour they killed in excess of three-hundred people – of which fifty-eight were minors – and injured over five-hundred others. By the next day their crimes would be considered insignificant; by the day after that their crimes wouldn't even be crimes.

Kaal ate at the usual times. He kept the pretence of order as if there were another kind, and he was almost never sick. The human saturation, sprawling and violent to no conceivable end below him, was no more a cause for disturbing his carefully managed equilibrium than say a bout of indigestion, or a stomach upset. He went about his routines in much the same way as he always had: all the pathetic automatisms of a rat dying in a bucket. Just because a quadrillion human beings and counting were in the process of decomposing, dying, or killing themselves, did not mean that he was any more absent to himself. His body continued to provide its own violence.

If he ever felt faint it was not as the result of any worldly deprivation, but rather because the world had been bequeathed to him and he had no use for it. To be alive in the morgue was shameless; but while his own composure sometimes seemed inscrutable to him, he also felt that what was going to happen had somehow already happened, and that all the future could threaten was the disclosure of this already suffered event.

This wholesale abjection was not new, just out of hiding, just scoped beyond former possibilities. For him, cocooned inside his Tower, it was both peculiarly tolerable and readily thinkable. It fascinated with all the seductive guile of a hyperrealized boredom: a boredom fascinated with itself. You'd think all the clambering bodies – bloated, dismembered, starved, exploded, bled out, rotting, frantic – would repulse and sadden anyone distant enough not to be panicked, and yet the spectacle proved too excessive for these sentiments, too maniacal to truly repel in any of the standard ways.

The mass oozed like some multicoloured discharge, a mutating culture grown from all cultures at once, from the wound of what it was to exist in the first place. His only devastation was insignificance. Always this way. An opacity of desperation now, maybe, that wasn't there before. Nothing more uncanny in this day-to-day than the unaltered flavour of his morning coffee. Nothing there to defile his heady sense of being removed from all this, aside from a certain gagging on himself that was always there. And yet he felt the altitude in his stomach and in his head. He was even woozy in his sleep. He almost wanted the bodies to deepen quicker, for the ground to rush to meet his falling stomach and then stop, for his escape never to have happened, because it couldn't go on: too sickly, too unreal, too dreamt up to have dreams of its own.

He saw many thousands of heads, of

children screaming, endless flows of people boarding empty freighters and aircraft carriers minus their airplanes. A sign above them read: EMERGENCY EVACUATION. The skyline, the port, the smoking debris of Chicago. A city-weight of voices: each one of them in a panic, each one of them some dialect of past and impending atrocity. Two gleaming white tugs trailed two black-hulled freighters out to sea. The camera zooming into the faces of those crushed into the railings at the edge of the ship. When they were far enough out that they could no longer be seen clearly by the hordes still streaming aboard other similarly destined ships, the railings collapsed and hundreds of humans at a time spilled over the edge into the sea. Clouds of nerve gas billowed from the deck subduing the thousands left there to the floor, to their deaths in the water. Figures in gas masks and protective suits emerged with silenced weapons to calmly dispose of what was left.

Almost all the video-feeds he watched were the same discordant melange of trauma: humans being shot, burned, stabbed, crushed, drowned, or else coming apart at different speeds. Those that endured, endured for more of the same: no end to it, ever. Only the dream of an end, of the final moral kill. And it's the dreamers that stay alive longest, which seems fair, being that they were still in many ways waiting to be born. As if this massacre wasn't just life. As if depravity wasn't just the straight path.

Defenestration was popular among the

unarmed and the untrained; particularly so, from the videos he'd watched, throughout Europe, China and Japan. With none of the uncomfortable intimacy of stabbing or strangling, it offered a favourable means of dispatch for those who, though conscientious, had no taste for killing. And there was always the distinct possibility that another death might be occasioned by the falling person landing on someone else at street level. Children were easier still, though the chances for these supplementary deaths were regrettably diminished. In sum, the toll on the population was only ever catastrophically small.

Outside of urbanizations, there was swamp and fire and animals drowned in mud, trees charred and snapped, rotted out bodies, the slime of the dead pooling in cattle tracks and the meandering ruts of old streams run dry. For weeks after, New Zealand remained nearly as verdant and unspoiled as before. But then the splitting accelerated and the planes came, dropping humans in their tens of thousands over its picturesque wilderness until almost all plant life was destroyed. The last footage he saw of this part of the world was of the Coromandel, from the air, turned grey.

He likened those outside to the strays

in the alleyways that used to border his house. Their howls and shrieks were so constant, so homogenous, that they seemed to emanate as if from a single animal, the suffering commensurate with its excessive mass. But of course *he* was now the stray, the deject, the outlier. Only, he was exiled not by deprivation but by comfort, and his being lost was in itself the most exalted form of opulence. He would try to ignore the condensing bodies on the ground by looking at the sky; and when it stormed, its blackened body lit up inside and growling, like a panther gorged on flashbangs, he'd sit and wait in silence for the rain. When it arrived he liked to see all those thousands of faces looking up into the downpour, their mouths open, eyes squinting, brains registering how not all the world was made of humans. How true it seemed then that oblivion had its own exquisite aspect, how caught in glimpses, freeze-framed, bursting in numerous punctums of wonder, it was the match for any creation.

He watched humans burnt alive in open pits, in mass executions, before anyone knew what mass meant. He saw the same humans days later exhumed by bombs. He saw them descend, saw them pulling dents out the earth, saw people coming apart in the air.

When flight was still possible, and hope for survival still widespread, half the world was made up of refugees: those from densely populated countries seeking their lesser populated versions, those from cities and condensed conurbations in search of wilderness and open land, and those from the countryside with designs on high-rises. It had to be better someplace else; the alternative was not worth thinking. The alternative, of course, though not worth thinking, was true: there was no place else – there was strict geographic location and its qualitative parity with every other place.

There was a remoteness to the woman's

eyes that went beyond the usual cerebral bruising, beyond the thousand yards of the war-deranged soldier and on and on without end – a distance that could never be retraced. Her expression didn't alter as she put the gun to her temple. It was like she'd stalled like that. The video slowed down as she pulled the trigger. The burst, the recoil, her head moving away and to the left, her expression unchanging. This composure of the already dead in the living was not rare, but somehow she, amid so many other examples, was not once surpassed. He looked for that look in the mirror, and knew that if he ever found it those hundred or so storeys would cease to make a difference.

Humans ran and ran until there wasn't

room to run, till the gasses of the dead pinched at their lungs, till the planet was an open grave, and its topographies precluded anything but staggering or crawling.

He watched the ground vomit and swallow itself over and over: a repulsive human fountain recycling its contents, absorbing more.

Humanity was abased as much by its imploded imagination as by the bits of freshly dead human it was forced to eat to stay alive. And so perverse that this universal solidarity should arrive only to find that this newly united thing must kill itself – for the sake of itself.

If women took it hard at first, like Tutsis raped and mutilated (breasts cut off, vaginas gouged out) on their way to be being killed, it wasn't long before just as many men found themselves permanently separated from their genitals. That the reproductive organs should have been targeted like this had, if anything, an old-world charm to it, given how the proliferation was determinably asexual. In the end, no prejudiced nuance, concerning race, gender, nationality, or sexual persuasion, could survive the sheer weight of people that needed to be made dead.

He watched unflinching as women, dripping in the blood of the babies they'd just butchered, prayed to God. How God must love all those tiny deconstructed humans made so quiet in the name of all that is good, he thought. He watched one woman give birth while people were eating her, starting on the baby before it had fully exited the mother. He watched and he waited to feel something. When it didn't come he felt the absence for as long as he could until that too went away.

In its proliferation, the human appeared memoryless. It had forgotten how the universe ignores it, and how the knowledge of that must be sublimated by ideals, by notions of progress, by aspirations of transcendence. All it had now was the continuing massacre and the vague sense that there existed a more human way to suffer.

Kaal had been a philosophy professor

at the University of Mumbai for about a year when they started digging out the foundations for the World Towers; and though he was based some distance away (at the Kalina campus, and lived nearby), he'd managed to visit the site most days. Of the three towers under construction, he'd always preferred World One to its neighbours, View and Crest. He would imagine himself inside it, at the top, imagine the quiet that could exist there.

Once he'd heard of a second and then a third documented split he knew somehow it wouldn't stop. He also knew where he had to get to, and that he didn't have long to get there. But then to say he knew did not quite capture what had happened, for he didn't know this as he knew other things: there was no rational process he could recall having gone through, only his body moving in certain ways and his then accommodating those movements by way of that conviction.

By the time the first video of a splitter became the most viewed video clip in history, just two days after its upload, he was already in the Tower. She was regarded by most as a unique case, not only the first but the last too, so that when more showed up there was the suspicion that the video was itself the primary catalyst for these subsequent splittings, as if the world was now in the grip of a Japanese horror movie – a rumour aided in its spread and supposed credibility by the girl's being of Japanese descent, although diasporic and resident at the time in São Paulo, Brazil.

Most of the isolated needed a cause.

They asked the same unanswerable questions, answered them in the same unanswered way. There was talk of everything from alien infection (making humans food for some forthcoming interplanetary invasion) to theoretical manifestations, such as the Lewisian overdetermination of persons being confirmed via some extraordinary biological shift. But as to why it was happening now and why to everyone at once, nobody had anything approaching a cogent explanation.

When he stepped out of the tired-looking

teaching block into the lunchtime choke of heat and bodies, having just delivered his final lecture ('On Kristevan Abjection: Apocalypse and the Double'), the campus, though ostensibly unaltered from all the other times, felt to him already like some diorama of the past.

The streets were never quiet, but as he walked in the direction of the Tower, a distance he'd usually never contemplate walking, right the way over to Mill Lands, he sensed the populace was somehow depleted. There were seconds of quiet between car horns, and more noise coming from the insides of buildings than was usual. The children weaving between the slow-moving traffic selling flowers sounded faint, as if underwater. A sequence of screams and a general quailing clamour issued from open windows and doors left ajar to facilitate the circulation of air.

The preparatory arrangements that would allow him access to the completed Tower, and a suitably positioned apartment within it, had been finalized two days before. A series of phone calls to various residents had been made, during which he'd offered an honorary degree from the University of Mumbai. Following a half-dozen failed attempts, an interview was arranged with a conveniently conceited multi-billionaire tech impresario, who'd had no trouble believing that he'd be in line for such an accolade, and if anything gave the almost unfathomable impression that its being tendered was somehow overdue.

As he walked, weaving his way between cars, motorbikes, other pedestrians, his legs took over. He wondered if it was possible to stop, to go in another direction, to turn back; and he thought he made the decision to try, just to see if he could, but nothing happened. He presumed that what had felt like a decision being made was merely an extension of his deliberation and not yet its conclusion. He tried not to think how much like a resolution it had seemed. He continued walking, speeding up, getting farther and farther away from that moment of wrongly perceived certitude and the place to where it ought to have redirected him.

The sound of car horns, the heat in waves across the roads, the endless food stalls with their brightly-coloured parasols, the bananas, the casaba melons, the wooden props and the bedraggled banners, the voices of men, women and children chewing at the front of his brain like a million microscopic grubs.

The abject authenticates itself through

necessity, through having no opposition, through answering

its own reluctance to exist: the whole world under the auspices of the self-pitying murderer, the murderer with no choice but to regard others as somehow symbolizing his own narcissistic demand that he be made once again present to himself.

Regardless of the production value, he

generally preferred the less stylized video clips, and tired of the GoPro POVs with their adopted personas and fantasy missions, those slaughter videos infused with heroic narratives filched from all over: the Bible, horror movies, historic battles, etc. Every circumstance, no matter how abominable, always attracts its enthusiasts, and in this case it was these howling morons frenziedly feeding YouTube with blood and dying faces while there was still time, soldiers of ill fortune carving paths through bodies like it meant something.

Uploaded from cities he presumed to be American were countless videos of people sniping from rooftops. Not just middle-aged men in checkered shirts and baseball caps, primed by zombie flicks to know that this was their one true calling, but humans of all ages, races, and genders. But then the spaces between bodies got filled up with more bodies and the chances of missing approached zero. And even when there were still heads to score from, it became increasingly difficult in the tumult for them to register their hits.

No matter how many times the makers of the videos mentioned their names, countries of origin, religious affiliations, they were all of them the same conscripted, anonymous instrument of death.

X shot Y ten times in the face, killing her.

A few moments later, as a crowd formed at the exit, X opened fire again, killing 23 more. X then began walking around the perimeter quoting Bataille out of context and urging the surviving members of the audience to kill themselves. One of X's former girlfriends claims that he was a tender and gentle lover: "He used to buy me gifts all the time. He was very generous. I never heard him raise his voice. Everything with him was romance." X had also doused all the livestock on a nearby farm with petrol and set them alight. The police arrived at 13.40, fifteen officers in total. When they tried to negotiate with X, he responded by shooting half of his remaining hostages in the genitals at close range. At 14.24, X shot himself in the head. He was found in a state of undress, with semen smeared across his thighs, dead yet still ejaculating at 14.54.

He watched a middle-aged man trying to resuscitate a young boy with a bicycle pump. The man was crying in a way that he had forgotten people cried. He was crying like he was starring in the movie version of his life. In the movie, he was the father and the boy was his son. The camera cut away to a dog eating the face off an old woman, over which the sounds of the man's hysteria could still be heard.

He will enter the apartment into a small

foyer at the west end of a long straight gallery that tapers off at its extremities. If he turns to his left he will enter the living and dining space, the dining table directly in front of him, and the sofa, TV and coffee table to his right. On his left will be a door leading into the servant's quarters, with its own kitchen area, storage room, bedroom, toilets and shower. On the south wall, there will be a sliding glass door leading out onto a private terrace. If he turns right at the foyer and follows the gallery north, he will find the doors to four bedrooms, each with their own en suite toilet and shower room, and sliding glass doors opening out onto the terrace. The open-air terrace will run the entire length of the apartment north to south in a curvilinear pattern (a stretched-out S), the largest section of which is situated outside the living and dining area and outside bedroom 1.

There will be 19 plants in pots on the terrace: 9 off the living/dining area, 3 off bedroom 1, 2 off bedroom 2, 3 off bedroom 3, and 2 off the master bedroom. When he arrives he will not know their botanical or common names. He will water them on instinct, when he senses the soil is sufficiently parched, or when the leaves are poised to wilt.

Equidistant from the planted spaces at each end of the terrace, off the living/dining area in front of the sliding doors, is a sun lounger in an upright position. Sitting there he will be able to see the terrace around him and the sky. That will be it. What he hears will be more than enough to fill the visual lacuna of what he will have to get up and walk forward three steps and lean over the edge to see: the roads, the buildings, the trees, the grass, or rather those things now overgrown with human bodies.

He will dress in the same clothes every day. In each of the five bedrooms (including the servant's quarters) there will be three sets of the same outfit, ordered on the first day from a clothing store nearby and delivered the same afternoon. There will be 15 pairs of dark grey 98% cotton 2% elastane trousers, 15 sepia brown cotton shirts with seven similarly coloured buttons up the front, 15 pairs of cotton black boxers, 15 pairs of thin grey socks (rarely worn), and 15 pairs of dark grey size-10 canvass shoes (rarely worn). Regardless of the temperature, he will always fasten all 9 buttons on his shirt.

He will sleep in all the bedrooms. One night in each on a strict rotation: servant's quarters, bedroom 1, bedroom 2, bedroom 3, master bedroom. In his sleep it will be as if he is asleep in all of them at once. Only on waking will a particular room arrive. He will have a laptop in every bedroom, and one in the main living/dining area. These will also be bought on that first day. The video software on all these machines will soon refuse to play anything but the files from a single folder (named "NFB"), remotely installed on the desktop of each.

Everything about the apartment will be luxurious and muted. Even the pieces of furniture that are quadrilateral in design will have their corners and edges dulled by tiny curves and the suggested immateriality of their pearlescent finish. Nowhere but from the sun outside will there be the threat of any glare, the spotlights and lamps spewing only a consistently ambient glow. The sheen on the hardwood floors will be similarly understated, and clouded here and there with the footmarks of the previous occupant. The walls will be covered in oversized tiles, in either tope or grey; which when he inspects them closely will reveal a delicately rendered craquelure pattern, evoking not so much aging as its superfluity. In the main living space, there will be a large corner sofa littered with scatter cushions. There will be low-level round tables at each end, and a thin oblong-shaped lamp on each. In the corner, behind the sofa, there will be a standard lamp in the same metallic finish. A rectangular coffee table at the same level as the seating will fill the space created by the L-shape of the sofa. Across the room, facing the corner point of the seating, there will be a 50-inch TV. A round ebony dining table with 6 chairs will be to the left of Kaal as he faces the TV, in a chair placed in front of it watching closely for something he feels he might miss from the other side of the room, in what amounts to a corner made of two intersecting curves. The ceilings will be set at a generous height. Where the long gallery space, which runs nearly the entire length of the property on its east side, enters this space, there will be floor-to-ceiling fretted screens made in ebony. The carpeting, underneath and around the sofa, the dining table, and the beds, will be a mottled beige, that from some angles will resemble chenille. He will live here for 195 days. When he leaves on the 195th day, he will not return.

There was no strategy of rubblization,

of desertification, only their inevitability. Scorched-earth campaigns were only feasible when you could envisage getting somewhere close to the earth. Anything organized enough to be called a war or a battle, or even a skirmish, in which some notion of provisional triumph might be established, had gone. Pieces of human skin stuck to the branches of trees like tired bunting, as if to mark the end of endings themselves.

He came to miss the factions, the armies, the militias, all the various collectives grounded in location or some tenuous likeness. In retrospect, he found their strained ideals and preservationist confidences oddly touching. And now they were all the same sludge. No separate tastes, no individual colours or shapes, just the beige gruel of things about to collapse. Just the amassment of the same. Just the meltdown of all humanity's rich variance into a tiresome slop.

The acme of his thinking would quickly

become his ability to circumvent thinking altogether. The calmness he'd managed to cultivate would go too far, and end up feeling like the impossibility of any recognizably human sensation. He would sometimes want to return to the panic and to the anxiety, to the threat of his being alive. The skin on his face will become punctated, his guts squirrely, as if the thoughts he refused to think were being thought elsewhere.

But none of this is completely new to him. He'd cured himself of neurosis in his twenties. He'd been terminally depressed back then, literally dying of it: bits of him falling away, his arms refusing to ferry food into his mouth, his jaws slackening into an infinite yawn. He'd cured himself through the exhaustion of fear. He'd overdosed to the point of near immunity. Afterwards, it was like he was living underwater. Like the fear was still there, on the surface of what he was now submerged in. Like he was anaesthetized. But to what and by what he couldn't say. You see, without the fear there wasn't anything. The fear had been the cage stopping him seeing how there was nothing outside it, and then there wasn't even that.

Since then only the unknown had sustained his interest, his respect. And given this trajectory it held no fear for him: if anything it represented the opposite of fear, the antidote even. If it wasn't known it wasn't liable to shrivel up and putrefy, glooping up his synapses, becoming a different, pernicious kind of unknown – that way too common indigestion of the brain.

It was now down to the isolated, down to him, to be human for all humans. Him: this non-assimilable alien, this monster sat behind a screen watching, only ever watching, as the congealed human animal tried and failed to consume itself.

All human life reduced to a binary

imperative: kill or suicide. The necessity to predate enshrined. Countries with the highest per capita ratios of private gun ownership were the most successful in this regard: USA, Switzerland, Finland, Serbia, Cyprus, Saudi Arabia… Every killer was a copycat killer. Either win or die, and virtually no one won. All the virtual-murderers could finally come out of hiding. And what could be more natural when a machine has taught you how to read, how to listen, how to see, how to be in a world that no longer resembles the world?

The more deaths you can claim responsibility for the more able you are to validate your existence. The more violence pacifies you the more attuned you are to your moral duty. There is no moral worth to mourning. Life must be sacrificed in the cause of life, life as the idealized state whereby there is less of itself: a sustainable life, a life choked no more by plenitude but by its own self-governance.

Spray-painted on the road across London Bridge in 6-foot letters were the following words and their partial redaction: "Humanity is overrated."

The Ballard Estate's recent excursion into
what could be mistaken for recreational violence made him think it should be re-baptized under the same name – one swapped initial being all it would take. Mumbai's little London was swimming in blood and smiles. The district's pre-eminent eatery was taken out yesterday at 17.45 by a pipe bomb, the crowd outside singing *Rule Britannia* among the flames and the smoke and the crudely dismembered bodies as if they'd already forgotten its Irani/Zoroastrian credentials and were shedding their colonial past instead. That this nationalistic gesture should occur now, when what little sense or meaning it might once have had was in such severe disrepair, was itself significant – reflexively so, as if to draw attention to the sense of bereavement felt over the passing of a possibility, however puerile.

Kaal was some too-tender age when his
mother died. There was only ever one of her. One unbranching limb and one ending of it. One tumour in one brain and only

one week to die. So many years for his father to die waiting for her to come back. And still waiting, or most likely dead. Such fussy deaths back then. So singular. So exophoric.

"You look different," said the man, who having opened the door to the full extension of his left arm, pulled it slowly back towards him.

"From what? We've never met."

"From your photograph. On the university website?"

"Oh, that. Old shot, bad likeness," Kaal said without hesitation, grinning.

Disarmed, the man opened the door and stepped out of the way, ushering him in and down the hall to his left. "Go in. Sit down. I'll be right with you."

Kaal knew the way. He passed the dining table to his left and sat down on the end of the large L-shaped sofa in the main living area. The glass doors leading out onto the terrace were open. Beyond them, in the middle of the outside space, was a sun lounger in an upright position. He imagined the view from there, planned to sit there when it was over.

The man returned, apologized for his absence, saying how he hadn't yet managed to organize any help, and asked if Kaal would like some refreshment.

Declining, he asked if he could use the toilet. Kaal got up, excused himself, and headed back in the direction of the front door, beyond which, on the opposite side, as he'd been informed (though he knew already), was a bathroom he could use. Once inside, he stood in front of the mirror above the sink. He studied the features of his face, wiped away the sweat beading on his brow and top lip. He looked at his reflection as if for reassurance. The question he asked was asked back. His face then answered itself without changing. He thought he sensed something move to his right. The showerhead leaked water for a few seconds and then stopped. He looked down into the toilet, flushed it and left the room.

His incapacity for anguish would become

his primary source of self-identification. It was his attempt at narcissism. He was daring this way, in this phobia towards thought, preserving a non-existence he was no longer entitled to. He'd developed a personalized brand of autism from his eschewal of fear, a depersonalization from the duplication of increasingly ineffectual persons. Funny that, if the humour hadn't gone as well – or become subordinate to detail, which amounted to the same thing.

An apocalypse does not end so much as

uncover. It's an epistemic revelation, a disclosure of secrets, a divine correction manifested in the world. It shocks us into submission, and from here we see how the world as we've imagined it falls away. The end of the world is no more than the end of the world's conforming to our cognizance of it. The apocalypse is the truth in a place that's systemically allergic to the stuff.

The long-awaited fall came as a glut, not a deprivation. Instead this bleak video game of the world. And for the few that had evaded its rebarbative dissonance, the new hikikomori, there was the wait for something else, and the growing disbelief that there could be anything there at the end of it.

Astronomers and physicists eulogizing over the resplendent wonders of the visible universe and its theoretical insides, like it was some cosmic fucking fairyland instead of a black hollowing expanse primed to pull you inside out, were examples of nature at its most ridiculous. It was as if they thought their brains greater than their own insignificance. All science's truths and enthusiasms make him icky, without exception.

Without the capacity for neurosis, the slump castes had always economized their pain to the moment, to the pain they were in, which was enough: there wasn't the energy for fancying how it might get worse, or better, or how their identities might not survive such eventualities. They did not speak in metaphors, they ate them instead. To observe the workings of their stomachs, their bowels, their intestines, was just to see semiotics at work at the biological level, at the level of the all-too-human that was somehow less than itself and better for it.

The disturbances of his life quickly became the familiar ones: indigestion, insomnia, lethargy, headaches. The screaming carpet of humans scurrying over themselves and growing in his direction became distant, like an alien war. But he could still remember what it was like before all this. He could remember 2 million under-fives dying in India every year, one every 15 seconds. And who would have imagined that wouldn't be enough? Not even close. Or that the street kids would outlive most of Mumbai's more affluent adults? What looked to him from his terrace like spasmodic human lava was to them an intricate maze of ever-shifting tunnels and networks, crawl spaces between bodies, legs, and arms, through the decaying versions lower down. Victoria Terminus was always the end of the line, and swarming with India's missing children: those frail little termites sniffing whitener in corners, washing in gutters, predated on by paedophiliac Fagins drunk on starvation and meths. Of Mumbai's 18 million inhabitants, half had been slum dwellers, barely salient even to themselves; and now it was as if the other half had caught whatever they had: a disease of disappearing, a sickness of vanishing by becoming more.

Rejoining his host in the spacious living

room, its Armani/Casa design equal parts chic and drab, Kaal sat down and opened his leather satchel, as if to retrieve the necessary paperwork. Instead, he pulled out his grandfather's old Enfield No.2 service revolver and some black cable-ties.

He sat there absentmindedly surveying the room.

According to the brochure and supplementary bumf he'd read, the décor was purported to be sympathetic to its location in the gateway to India, and yet he couldn't see it. If anything it was the antidote to Mumbai's worst excesses. The apartment's curvilinear layout was perhaps the only true concession to Indian architecture, a nod perhaps to the Buddhist stupas of the Post Maha Janapadas period, but could just as easily be assimilated from the Indo-Islamic blend of the mosques built in the Mughal period. Or the Ajanta caves even, at a stretch. In short, the apartment was the perfect vantage point from which to watch the world go under, providing as it did the nowhere in the view from nowhere. And already there was the sense of his gradually fading to nothing, of the sentence to come, and of the inescapable inevitability of something he didn't yet understand.

North of the railway tracks, a lower level

building had collapsed under the weight of clambering bodies: so many mangled limbs and punctured bellies, so many crushed skulls, so many people already half-dead invigorated by fresh agonies.

Even as they were dying it was hard for them not to believe they were just acting in a movie, or else in the process of respawning in some first-person shooter. The alternative was that this was all real, and the mind-crushing insanity of that.

A puritan killing spree, in which life itself was deemed impure, was at least honest, was at least accurate. Once you've killed your own son, daughter, wife/husband, mother, father, as some did, what was left of killing? The rest were just validations of those familial murders. The rest weren't just easier, they were your only reason for being alive. The perversion though was not this, but everything that had gone before it. It took on a retrospective perversity. The perversion was suffering yourself in the absence of others, all the many experimented realities, our directionless directions, our aimless circling of the dream of progress. It was not this but the waiting for this that was perverse.

The persistence of a single referent, this

me this *him* this *same thing*, this object for no one, was fetishistic, was phobic, was bitten by a diseased mouth. His life was now just the deprivation of the dreams he'd had for it. This mesh of some 30,000 afternoons, or thereabouts, at best, at worst. How slowly we die before we die, and how quickly thereafter. Ha, funny mirage this life: devoured, devouring, always hungry – never there until it isn't.

Between the tranquility of where he sat

and the hysteria of the ground swell, there was a shrinking area of speculative liquescence (an interspace) that was experientially resistant in its detail to anything but fear on the one side and blinded growth on the other. This area, only demarcated in order that it induce anxiety in the party thereby encroached upon, is where he went to in an effort to exist. He put himself there in a desperate attempt to feel something other than his own preprogrammed responses. If he came alive at any time in this now routine meditation, he didn't notice it happening.

Identity was the opposite of authenticity, always had been. To be human on earth was to experience diaspora – to have it become your identity, to identify with the nowhere of everywhere at once. He'd taught it and now he was living it.

He read of many hundreds of thousands

of men, women and children being encouraged to take refuge in forests, and incendiaries being dropped on them by planes. Such practices were used across Australia, the Upper Midwest of the USA, California, Alaska, Russia, and Greece. Millions died. But the fires stopped. And so many millions more did not die, and became more and more and more, until there were no forests left to burn, until the tallest trees were underfoot, until layer upon layer of poorly combustible human bodies was all that was left.

He watched the faces below him looking up at the sky like it was their friend, as if what was above them could only ever be a place of enchantment, pending some promised relocation.

"Humanity reproduces itself like kipple.

There is no winning against this relentless proliferation. Humans are obutsu, unclean, waste to be cleared to make way for an unpolluted, crystalline era of the purely digital: a world of proxy gods who live elsewhere, whose compulsive need to eat from the planet has been quelled by the inexhaustible virtuality of reconstituted space." Was this Félix Guattari's chaosmosis? The decoding of chaos into the infinite other of the virtual? The chaoide of our imaginations under siege? Oneiric hypostatization, recombinant flux, anomic precarity, spasmodic fractalization, depersonalized space...? Kaal couldn't work it out. The more he listened to the man on the screen the more lost he became.

The man sat in the armchair with his

wrists and ankles bound. He was looking at Kaal with a disbelief ordinarily reserved for ontological anomalies, or for the kind of discrepancies in time and space that ungrounded the veracity of consciousness itself. Kaal had been explaining what was coming, predicting all that was about to happen, and the man just watched him talk, the way you'd watch an avalanche you have no hope of outrunning. Kaal thought the man might wet himself, but to his credit he managed to mostly keep it together. He couldn't understand that what Kaal was doing was moral before its time. There was no convincing him. He kept saying how the building's security would arrive soon and how Kaal should leave while there was still time, that you don't pay the amount he paid for this place and run the risk of just anyone getting in. It seemed unnecessary to point out that the problem of getting in had already been solved, but Kaal did it anyway. The man kept saying how there'd be checks and how there were procedures in place, and Kaal continued to detail how the future was about to fall apart. When Kaal mentioned how if he threw him off the terrace now it would still be possible for him to hit the ground directly, the man stopped talking.

"I can't watch this," the man on the screen told anyone willing to watch, which at the time of Kaal's viewing ran into millions. He was in his twenties, looked as if he hadn't slept in a week, or laughed since he was a child. He picked up two Biros from the desk in front of him and plunged them into his eyes. That he actually imagined this would reduce his suffering was something worth noting. The comments section indulged the usual simpleminded opprobrium: those that wished they'd performed the same clumsy operation before watching it, the interminably shockable, the despisers of any weakness that dared to masquerade as a strength, the usual anonymous jokers and puritans whose rampant commentary continued uncurbed.

That there were still people writing responses to videos, that this was likely the last literature, made him think of a passage from Kristeva's *Powers of Horror*:

On close inspection, all literature is probably a version of the apocalypse that seems to me rooted, no matter what its socio-historical conditions might be, on the fragile border (borderline cases) where identities (subject/object, etc.) do not exist or only barely so – double, fuzzy, heterogeneous, animal, metamorphosed, altered, abject.

And that the apocalypse had already come and gone was not, of course, lost on him, it being almost a platitude by then; but there was yet something of the threat of it that remained, and it remained with him, inside the predicted weakness of his being human, that he too would come to see these once gloriously pointless innovations as nothing more than a deified uselessness, elevated not by some mercurial system of merit, but by a confluence of malformed luxury and ill-conceived hope.

"Human overpopulation impairs the lives

of humans, for while there's an increase in intimacy, and intimacy is a good thing for humans, it's the wrong kind of intimacy. The right kind is the kind you enjoy. But then the enjoyment of a life is quite probably meaningless anyway. It needs only to be lived – and not even that. Overpopulation is numbers and more than numbers: after all, it's the express depletion of environment and non-renewable resources that further exasperate the human want for comfort. All the humans I see are bubbling like fizzy drinks, and fizzy is a happy condition, but theirs is a different kind – the fizz sulfuric acid makes as it eats into a person's skin. The ratio of births to deaths is crucially important: a significant imbalance here will not be sustainable. Starvation, too, you might think, is a particularly bad thing when it leads to the eating of other humans, but this needn't be the case. Malthus (with his "preventative" checks to limit reproduction, and "positive" checks in the guise of war and disease) didn't see that humans were their own resource and could potentially outgrow the threats of their environment. Human overpopulation has not been caused by this recent mutation, only aggravated. When this began, there were more humans in India than were on the entire planet in 1900. We remember when 16 million was the upper limit. Tertullian was concerned for the people of Carthage. Confucius, Plato, Aristotle: all worrywarts in this regard. Remember when they educated themselves into lesser numbers so they could have all those unborns' consumables for themselves? 7-odd billion seems like as many lifetimes ago. The war method is failing: every human at war with every other human and yet population growth continues to accelerate. Children die at record levels and still no slowing down. And who has time to wait for the old diseases to mutate? (The ideal diseases would be brought from another planet, a disease for which we wouldn't possess the slightest immunity.) A plague, unprecedented in scale, is perhaps the best we can hope for, but then… well, then what? Sub-Saharan Africa was already crawling all over itself and now there's a body for every limb and only the prospect of more. Remember when they were concerned about an extra 200,000 humans every day? More than 70 million new people every year, and then, within weeks, 7-odd billion became close to 15 billion, more than half of them concentrated in ten countries: China, India, United States, Indonesia, Brazil, Pakistan, Nigeria, Bangladesh, Russia and Japan. And in the weeks it took global life expectancy to plummet (67, 66, 65, 64, …), 15 billion becomes 30 billion. And whereas migration had served to supplement countries with low birth rates, migration and countries themselves are found to be increasingly irrelevant. There are only humans piled on top of other humans, the distinction between urban and rural now no more than a painful anachronism. Some cities, though, can still be distinguished by their scrapers, and the high-rise shanty towns that are forming in their upper levels. By numbers alone, the Cotswolds is no less a hypercity than greater Tokyo. The whole of Iceland turned into Ho Chi Minh City. Further technological advance, ordinarily coincident with population swells and an increased demand for food, is only exasperated by the current abundance of humans. Whereas newborns would ordinarily perish under these conditions (poor sanitation, scarcity of suitable foods and medicines) these are not your standard newborns. Splitters are a new-fangled scourge, replicating older methods to greater effect: their split-rate appearing to accelerate in response to these increased threats. With population growth rates and fertility rates exceeding all previously recorded levels, the death rate, though high, cannot keep up. The ecological footprint has become the stomp of a boot thick with effluence. Complete deforestation looks imminent as humans turn beaver for sustenance. 1968 saw the publication of *The Population Bomb* (an alarmist neo-Malthusian bestseller) written by Professor Paul R. Ehrlich and Anne Ehrlich. The book argued that agricultural production rates would fall short of population growth. Up until the definitive explosion, although the population had continued to rise, the numbers of those undernourished had actually fallen drastically, thus discrediting its central thesis. And while a lack of available food did indeed become an issue when the real bomb went off, no amount of agricultural growth or ingenuity would remedy it. The solution, as far as it qualified as one, demanded a level of immediacy that the Ehrlichs could not have credibly imagined. In 2017 obese humans outnumbered malnourished ones. China had an "obesity surge," while almost half of India's children were malnourished. On a global scale, food supply is thought to determine population, an increase in the former leading inevitably to an increase in the latter. As if in response to lack of food and water, splitting only becomes more frequent. A shortage of potable water, however, is perhaps our best hope. Water tables have been falling for years. A human requires 2 litres of drinking water per day. We would need to desalinate the oceans. The Jebel Ali Desalination Plant (Phase 2) in the United Arab Emirates was the world's largest desalination plant, producing 300 million cubic metres of water per year, or approximately 2500 gallons per second. Now, when it is most needed, it is no longer in operation. Until very recently, with a new approximation of 1-3%, scientific estimates on the human occupation of the Earth's total surface had never exceeded 1%. This percentage has increased exponentially since the first split, with the inhospitality of given regions – the mountains, the poles, the deserts, the oceans – fast becoming insignificant. The human explosion arrived and has not stopped exploding…" There was another hour of this man's rambling polemic, but Kaal couldn't listen to any more. His head reeled with the detail of it, with the manifest futility of such a drawn-out itemization of the sickness crawling up his outside walls.

The new spatial ambivalence of the human

lent itself to death with an inevitable ease. When your head's togetherness felt like a prank, what could be more natural than to have it spread across a wall, to have it rot there in the sun, and to still exist somewhere else in spite of that?

He could hear motivational speeches being broadcasted from the tops of scrapers, from helicopters and the occasional hot air balloon. The voices used sounded not unlike pre-fission-era adverts for skin rejuvenation creams, shampoo, sanitary products.

He thought he smelled horses burning in the harbour. There were hundreds of boats in the water, each one overloaded, rocking precariously, bodies overboard with every swell, the clouds of smoke above their heads the colour of fresh bruises. Availing themselves of all and any boat, he watched them heading for the islands, Butcher and Elephanta. They amassed there and fought off new arrivals with rocks and sticks, and guns if they had them. Drownings were commonplace. The bay began to fill with bodies.

Before shooting the former occupant in the stomach, Kaal had managed to extract (and to verify) enough of his bank details to make his staying in the Tower indefinitely not only feasible but a prospect that looked like being, at least for a time, luxurious beyond his habits or his needs. He'd retracted all his earlier talk about multiplying bodies and the planet's accelerated choking to death, dismissing them as some twisted levity on his part, and the man had seemed relieved. This relief was reinforced when he told him how his real purpose was money, a subject the man understood and thereby a motivation he could at last assimilate. Kaal was quick to get as much information as he could before this newfound calm turned to indignation, which it did, but too late then to matter.

"We become truly abject only as we come to know that which has been hidden from us, for reasons we still fail to understand. If we could know the hidden's reason for having been hidden and its reason for no longer being so, we might yet rid ourselves of this sense that we have been defiled, and so discover a purity hitherto unsought by all but saints and madmen. But this seeking is asymptotic. We dirty ourselves with it. We: the revenants of our decayed curiosity lazily piggybacking on our heartbeats.

"The first time you see a famous landmark submerged in humans it disorientates: The Statue of Liberty up to her armpits in scrambling bodies, The Kremlin barely recognizable but for the flag waving from the Palace's golden pole, Big Ben's face maculate as if with flies…" The man wanders around what looks like his bedroom gesticulating wildly. When he comes up close to the camera it becomes easier to see that his eyes are not blinking, and that his mouth, partially buried behind a beard stained yellow with cigarettes, is completely out of synch with what he is saying.

Even with food and water enough to sustain him indefinitely, the possibility of his staying alive for more than a year was limited to a few highly improbable outcomes: (1) the divisions coming to an abrupt end, and the tide of humans as a consequence plateauing till eventually it subsided; (2) a plan of mass clearance being put into operation by whatever organization remained with whatever technology they might have left at their disposal; (3) someone arriving in a microlight or a helicopter, landing on the roof and offering transportation to a location more suited to his continued existence. There were these and perhaps more he had missed, and of course an abundance of far more fanciful possibilities that he had neither the time nor the residual imagination to consider.

He watched a car disappear beneath a swamp of bodies. The way they rubbed up against each other sounded like frogs. When the car was half-submerged there was a pause. The middle of the roof was the last visible part of the sinking vehicle. For a second or two, he thought he heard the buzzing of a plane, but when he looked up there was nothing there.

In a basement flat behind multiple layers

of reinforced boarding, a family of three – mother, father, son – lay on their backs on a mattress on the floor. The mattress was stained the colour of teabags at various stages of becoming dry, and from it they each stared up at the ceiling, wide-eyed as if dead, as if their still heaving chests had forgotten that it had happened. The noise from outside was clamorous and included screams and loud, angry-sounding voices speaking words he couldn't make out but recognized as Japanese. Although the ceiling wasn't visible, the abject manner in which they stared in its direction led him to believe there was something more there than the usual expanse of painted plaster.

A new stream showed an ugly refrain

of middle-aged white men jumping off tall buildings. Indian farmers had been killing themselves, ten a day, for decades. Suicide for them was already a way of life. To hear that Monsanto's executives and their like were now doing the same thing must've been, he thought, quite the despairing joy.

Some appeared to experience an almost maternal anguish, as if watching something die over and over again was somehow evidence of their having at one time given birth to it, as if what was once inside them had been ripped out to be dissected over and over, its insides multiplying into an outside it could not fill.

Next on the screen were young boys built like small birds climbing up the backs of men to cut their throats. The boys were gone, onto the next, before the men had even considered the senselessness of trying to put their necks back together. They swarmed over the crowd, some supernatural species made for stealth and speed and the cleanest of unclean murder. The perverse jouissance of this diluvial normality was not lost on him, all of it evincing a strangeness that repulsed with its excess, with its becoming everyday.

He recalled a quote from Kristeva, words he'd read out on that last day at the university, understanding them then in a way he'd never understood them before, feeling their prescience inside him like a curse: "Provided we hear in language – and not in the other, nor in the other sex – the gouged-out eye, the wound, the basic incompleteness that conditions the indefinite quest of signifying concatenations. That amounts to joying in the truth of self-division (abjection/sacred)."

He spent the first few days in the Tower

catching up on the latest footage of human fissioning. In their first instances, filmed splittings were not only scarce and poorly executed, the camerawork being so hysterical in its movements as to induce vertigo in the viewer, they were also of questionable origin. These dubious productions would mimic the tremulous images and bad light of those videos already online and were hard to discern from the real thing. As the recordings became more commonplace, however, the poise and clarity improved to such an extent that it was almost as if all the earlier examples were faked somehow, and that their failings served only to disguise this common stratagem.

The scission disorder, mutation, disease, or PRS (perennial rupture sickness) as it came to be known for a short time, differed from birth in that its functional variance was considerable. The chances of seeing two cases the same were slight, and so it seemed fair to conclude that dissimilitude of process was symptomatic of the condition. The main points of divergence were in the locality of extrusion and exit, the relative mass, the congruity of form between product and producer, the concentration and degree of trauma, the motility and verbalizations of the product, its emotional impact, and the duration of the episode.

Sometimes there was just the arrival and nothing else: no apparent procedure of emergence, no physiological rending or distension, just two bodies where there was once one. The apparent physical independence of the product in these cases led to theories postulating remarkable advances in the science of hard light, advances responsible for the phenomenon of PRS in its entirety. That humans should just start multiplying on this model ran counter to all received biological understanding and was therefore considered metaphysically impossible; and so its *apparent occurrence*, a phrase whose dyadic form had been ruefully neglected, need not, they thought, constitute the epistemic catastrophe many had first thought, for it did not necessitate that the scientific community incorporate the latter, but instead understand the possibilities for the former's causal and existential priority. We should then forgo, the argument went, explaining the occurrence in favour of explaining it away, explaining it as nothing more than a misstep of ontological presupposition. Citing the findings of certain Princeton engineers as the genesis of these hard holograms, advocates of this position went on to mention others working in the field and numerous government programmes associated with the military application of these incredulous technologies.

However misguided the theories, Kaal enjoyed all the many expositions on what was happening. He also could not stop watching all the myriad faces of the event itself. He spent entire days in front of his screens, often forgetting to eat, falling asleep upright in chairs, waking as if to the shock of being alive.

In a privately-constructed bunker in the

garden of a bungalow in North Dakota, an overweight man in a suit sat eating from a tin of baked beans. He ate them one by one as if to savour something he knew could never be repeated. Over the course of the five-minute time-lapse video, he became at least as many versions of himself as beans consumed. He consumed the space like prions in the brain of a deer.

"We had only half-existed and now have

gone from needing 1.5 similar-sized planets to absorb our waste to needing an entire solar system. Even our smallest countries need a planet to themselves. But there isn't time to make plans for the Kuiper belt, or to get anywhere else (Venus,

Saturn, Uranus, Neptune…) in large enough numbers to make a difference. John S. Lewis's *Mining in the Sky* claimed that our own solar system can support 10 quadrillion humans. Stephen Hawking has said that "our only chance of long-term survival is not to remain inward-looking on planet Earth but to spread out into space." Powell's StarTram, with its projected 4 million per decade per facility, wouldn't be enough either, and then there's the length of the flight and the duplication in transit. Arthur C. Clarke and Isaac Asimov didn't regard this exodus into space as a viable solution – convinced that the problem would begin and end here, on Earth – and neither do I…."

At an intimate gathering of prematurely

aged teenage hideaways, some miles west of some place mentioned but improperly heard, a sacrifice, séance or some such ritual was about to commence. The five of them sat in a circle, an arm's-length between each, three males and two females, their heads downcast, their hands in their laps. There were occultist-looking symbols painted on the bare floorboards and a knife in the middle with a curved blade. One of the girls lifted her head and looked at the other four in turn. Her nose had been chewed off and the lobe of her left ear was missing. Two of the five were quaking as if petrified or stifling laughter. The camera was operated by a sixth individual, also female, who slowly circled the gathering in an anticlockwise direction. It was her that spoke at the beginning, whose nervy voice unravelled on any words with more than two syllables.

The room was lit by a single lightbulb hanging from the ceiling, off centre to the right of the human ring, and conspicuously bright. There was the sound of breathing and a hundred or more cars honking and idling at an uncertain distance. The breath of those seated on the floor formed into small clouds. These clouds took on the shape of humans, humans that killed the humans from whose breath they'd just materialized by growing so large as to remove all the air from their bodies and from the rest of the room.

A little girl, about five years old, hung from her neck from an overhead cable in a suburb of Detroit. Far from dead, she sang loudly enough for residents to hear for two or more blocks. Even after the neck gave way and the body became separated from the head, she could still be heard singing from the cable. The wolves underneath that were eating from her stomach looked up at where the voice was coming from, distracted, touchingly so, from their sustenance for a few seconds, as if the acclivity of their muzzles was a kind of prayer.

Other species (those not already made

extinct, and he remembered the Atlas Bear, the Caribbean monk seal, the Bluebuck, the Falkland Islands wolf, the Yangtze dolphin, the Black rhinoceros) died alongside the humans in the crush, or else the humans ate them, or else they lived on the humans, the dead versions and the live ones. In the short term, whatever the variations, dead things were not without utility. It allowed the construction of huge artificial islands, like those already in existence off the coast of the United Arab Emirates and the Emirate of Dubai, to increase a thousandfold. The reclamation of land lost to the sea was also stepped up. The ballast used was human and animal bodies. Time-lapse footage showed the seas and oceans shrinking like a puddle drying in the sun.

The humans he saw seemed locked in

a kind of tyranny of the moment. Was as if what thoughts they had now stood alone, impregnable, refusing the former connectivity that had allowed for the formation of complex sequences. All but this here now was the purest ambivalence. Nothing but this same life lived differently, or else this different life lived just the same. Such a dreary fucking cataclysm: this end-of-the-world which, after all, did not end.

The man on the screen had a beard that

had grown right up around the bottoms of his eyes. He chewed at an area on his top lip that was used to being chewed, that had hardened as a result and did not bleed. The room around him was his equal in dishevelment. When he spoke, his mouth was barely visible behind the thick covering of facial hair: "We're seeing the creation of an oil planet. Spaceships will come and collect the bodies and transport them in drums the size of countries. The question is why these advanced societies still need oil: perhaps for plastics, or as plant fertilizer. Or if not aliens then the superrich. And while it takes many millions of years for oil to form, maybe… maybe a method of accelerating the formation of fuels from animal matter has been secretly devised and…" By the end of the transmission, both his eyes were rotating in their sockets.

The panic to bury the dead quickly, when it was feasible, when people could be organized to do such things, when there was still earth free of bodies to dig, had little or nothing to do with hygiene, disease control, or maintaining some kind of aesthetic equilibrium, and everything to do with the formation of oil. Else why bury all the dead plant life in with them too? The planet was to become the largest oil reservoir in the solar system. All of this devised by aliens. Or so his theory went, and he'd heard similar from others.

The future arrives: the entire planet, a single terrain, gases seeping through the gaps between the dead, to be set alight, monolithic spumes of fluffy yellow-orange fire churning dense inky smoke like a Kuwaiti oil field (man's precious black bile purified with flames).

The video screens on the buildings in New York, Seoul, Tokyo, Hong Kong…, reflected the crowd back at itself. There was nothing else left to advertise but man's consumption of himself.

The human narrative had become trans-

parently senseless, had succumbed to the illogic of a dream, a dark vision, a new impossibility of truth, and of solution, and of history. The inexorable banality of chaos. Nobody had the audacity for words. There were shrieks and grunts and screams and gasps, all the confused and stench-ridden orgasms of death, but the languages were gone, all slobber and shit, replaced by the abjection of their exteriorized emptiness, by the decay falling through into the third and fourth floor windows of tower blocks: a hideous para-human sound. The abyss was with him wherever he went, the abyss was stuck to the bottom of his feet, and flabby and rotting there, the stench of it grown thicker than the entire world's accumulating dead.

The apartment, for all its metal, glass, wood

and fabrics, was a metaphor, a figure of speech denoting the object it would like to be but was not. All day long he heard it talking, convincing itself that of the concrete places in the world that exist it is one of them, and not merely an exaggeration masquerading as one, an overstatement of its own understatement.

There were moments when he felt the building becoming flimsy to the point of collapse, and was sure he could feel it swaying, as if both the exertions of the thronged, and the percolating decompositions of the dead, were gently rocking it to and fro, gradually weakening its structural integrity minute by minute.

She had that now trademark autocue stare, and spoke with a voice that could have been anyone's: "Who'd have thought our insides were so filthy as to contain the algorithms for this self-dissemination. The biblical exhortation, that it is what comes out of man and not that which goes into him which is the true source of his defilement, has been literalized beyond the doctrinal fancies of even the most seditious of exegetic scholars.

"If the impurity of man does not enter from without, but is, as Christ has told us, in him from the start, then what is this proliferative orgy but the releasing of that impurity (the devil cast out), and man's seeking to hide it again, amongst the acids of his belly? Seems odd to pity it, but our stomachs are only so big. We are all of us complicit in this amoebic displacement of our failed identities, the reality of which has indeed proved stronger than death.

"Societal and religious taboos surrounding anthropophagy, formed over many thousands of years, are being overcome in just so many days, the eating of one's own fission product, where possible, becoming the preferred option: an ameliorative process of resorption whereby the division could be seen to be undone, expiated even. Incest, cannibalism: the taboos fall together. As I have heard, 'If you've raped your sister, you may as well eat her too.'"

She paused. A leprous, bubbling discharge began spurting from her eyes. She struggled to speak as her throat and mouth were filling with the same pus-coloured liquid. The substance aggregated in mid-air to form the shape of another woman.

A vlogger in his late teens was animated

to the brink of falling off his chair and into the screen. He convulsed so violently the live feed freeze-framed him blurred, so violently the lag sometimes had his face appear on the back of his head, or the side, or up and over to the right where there was no head, only a face all twisted up with itself till it caught up with its body and spoke: "Time to wake the fuck up, morons! David Lewis was right! Speculation's over. The logic of our language is king and this swarming fucking turd of a planet of ours proves it. We were two or more people all along. The people we become are two or more people and the ones they become are four or more people and so on and so on. Our identity and our psychology are reconciled his way. There's no fission problem, only two or more people becoming spatially distinct. We've been counting ourselves incorrectly all this time. Our assumptions were wrong, which put our calculations out. That's all this is. We were counting spatio-temporal coincidence and not the persons themselves. Things do not just arrive out of nowhere. All these people made of spumes of blood of clouds of breath were all there already, only we didn't see them. And it was an understandable mistake, because how were we to know this would happen? And those that argue that our ontological status now cannot depend on some future event need to update their physics. The future travels backwards, fucktards, and we are each of us legion and always have been. The time to die is never! The time is always, over and over. The time…" His eyes filled with smoke. He stabbed himself in the face with a kitchen knife until the blade got stuck and he couldn't get it out. He was still wrestling with it when he expired.

Beneath the humans he could see, swarming

over each other as if there was nothing more to life than continuing to move at all costs – to kill, to avoid death, to eat – lay an ever-thickening underlay of corpses turning liquiform. As the dead bodies piled up they became totemic, became a symbol of common purpose, less the abomination and increasingly the single and sacred object representing all human majesty and drama, the coagulated altar to and of mankind's eternal sacrifice. The dead's metonymy as a symbol of life. And what remained but the humans that survived in spite of that survival, those abominable in their not yet being dead, while at the same time embodying what was left of human possibility.

A woman looked into the camera, the

centres of her eyes twitching like bugs trapped in spider webs, her mouth moving with no sound. There was nothing behind or around her: her face taking up the entire frame. He watched waiting for what was going to happen. Tiring of her inactivity, he slid the timeline bar twenty minutes to the right, two minutes short of the end. Nothing was different. He slid the bar back to the left, checking for things he might have missed. There was only the face looking back unaltered and the insinuation of some impending change. He slid the bar back where it was, watched the last two minutes. In the closing seconds the sound of torrential rain, or a shower coming on, and reflected in her pupils, stilled for a moment – where before there'd been nothing, not even the camera – the same image of her own face.

The human thing, amorphous now, was

growing like an accelerated moss, devouring itself in order that there might be more of itself to devour in the future. Its hostility towards its own mass inexhaustible, an inestimable reserve matched only by its rate of escalation. But as it grew its density decreased, becoming increasingly airy, honeycombed, discarnate – as porous and gauzy as the poorest slum kid.

Eyes viscid, bulging and discoloured like slugs, the mouth half-open, the lips gluey and oddly askew, the nose inflated at the nostrils to the point where the skin had become almost transparent, the veins like tiny red roots clearly visible beneath the skin, the brow the cheeks the pallor of pruned feet, glassy with sweat, the entire countenance sunken like the bone underneath was in the process of softening: the screen a portrait of the universe's incalculable horror crammed inside a human skull.

He'd been inside the Tower for about a

fortnight. It was the second week in June: monsoon season. The downpours were increasing in severity by the day. This year it found Mumbai's inhabitants already drowning in themselves. Drowning like those plaster icons of Ganesh dropped into the sea. He remembered all those smiling Pipe-Yard kids swimming in shit-filled, malarial water, in petrochemicals and scunge and rat piss, and there was already something unmistakably Edenic about it, given what was coming.

Since entering the Tower he'd avoided all contact with anyone else in the building. He had though been informed of their plans to quarantine the top two floors, via a detailed note attached to his front door. Apparently, other floors were doing the same, so that the entire block would soon be divided up into a series of hermetically sealed layers. Those in the lower half of the building had already evacuated to occupy residences farther from the ground. All stairwells and lift shafts had been blocked with thousands of litres of expanding foam that hardened to form a mass more impenetrable than the bricks that surrounded them. Pre-empting the inevitable power loss, generators had been rigged up in haste to supply the isolated apartments with electricity – enough, so he was informed, to run the standard appliances etc. for at least one year.

His stockpile of food and bottled water was considerable by then. He'd spent the first day or so ordering supplies, while they were still there to order. After filling the apartment's two large freezers, and buying another one and filling that too, he'd concentrated on dry foods, such as lentils and rice, and canned goods. The plan was to use the tap water until it was cut off, or became contaminated, and then move on to his bottled supply.

Although there was no room for the men

and women there to cast their shadows, he could still just about make out the rough outline of Ken Smith's scaled-down, fun park interpretation of the Nymphenberg Palace's grand parterre, its multi-coloured grasses, arboreal podiums, its tennis and basketball courts, its five acres of lotus pools and fountains, its full verdant overload.

Every swimming pool was filled with bodies seeking refuge from the sun. The spa's once soft sedation, there to lavish the senses with its own expensive brand of tranquillity, was now a frenzied fight for space, rejuvenating no one it seemed but Kaal. The Lodha dream had soured the instant someone crapped into one of its pools. What use anyway was equanimity that fragile? This kind of forced environmental calm never worked for long; if you wanted wellbeing on tap then narcotics were the only route. All these halcyon contrivances ever did for Kaal was make him more antsy. It was almost a relief for him to see it covered in thin ragged bodies, its pools filling with shit, its plants trampled into the ground.

From the time he'd first seen it completed, its sterility had ungrounded him. It was as if he was watching a promotional video for the clinically bored. Simulated men and women strolled along the pathways of simulated gardens appearing to talk amiably about subjects of passing consequence, and, as if secured to their continued amusement by only the finest of threads, completed their perambulations merely to resume them again elsewhere, as part of a presumably infinite sequence of such pleasures, with no one instance ever proving sufficiently convincing on its own.

On the fourth occasion one morning of

someone knocking at his door, and irked by the interruptions, he tucked his pistol into the back of his trousers and opened the door.

"नमस्ते," said the man, a septuagenarian who was doing his best to look much younger.

Kaal replied in English in the hope that the man would either insist on Hindi, or have no choice but to insist on it, so removing any obligation to talk.

As he stood there in front of him, without the distortion of the fisheye, he noticed something familiar about the old man: his gammy right arm, his eyes bulbous, set too far apart, conspicuously ranine. He said his name was Sanchit, said it as if Kaal would need it for future reference, as if they'd talk again often and he would use it and some difference would be made.

Kaal looked out into the corridor and waited for the man to say whatever it was he'd arrived there to say.

"You know, it's like Bombay in reverse."

"What's that?"

"What's happening. It's like the seven islands artificially grown together over the 18th and 19th centuries, the sea in between them reclaimed to give us the city we're in."

"It's everywhere though."

"But we're here."

"So what?"

"It matters where we are. It's relevant. We have more and richer billionaires here than anywhere."

"Billionaires of what?"

"It's what that type of person attracts, what builds up around them, that matters."

Kaal laughed with such obvious derision the old man could not mistake his contempt for anything else. "What, like sycophants?"

The old man's head executed the slowest of bobbles.

Having nothing else to say, Kaal made random symbols on the thick hardwood door with his right index finger, conveying, he thought, if the old man bothered to notice, which he didn't, the perfect mixture of nonchalance and mild impatience.

"You haven't divided?"

"There a fifty more back there," Kaal smiled, which surprised him, barely recognizing the sensation.

"We have to help each other. If it happens. When. We need to help each other dispose of them. There'll be no room. The food and water will run out. We should have it worked out in advance."

"Sometimes they're virtually indistinguishable. How will I know it's not you I'm throwing over the top?"

The old man went to speak and stopped.

Kaal smiled again and started to close the door.

"We should think of a way to escape. We can't last here forever. Wait…"

On his way back to the terrace Kaal thought about the old man's use of the word "forever" and shook his head despairingly.

If the Apollo Bunder was a scene at the

best of times it was now thousands of scenes all swarming over each other, becoming one scene, becoming a wailing blend of brightly coloured shirts and blood and panic. The Lashkar-e-Taiba bombs would have registered at this point as little more than a sneeze.

At the harbour end, the coagulated bodies had reached the roof of the Gateway's central dome and continued to rise. There were already people on and around the turrets. They were leaning over the edge and pulling up others, friends or family members, in the belief most likely that they could wait it out there, as if whatever was happening would stop happening at some point in the near future, and they would make their descent and walk away. It was a lamentable spectacle: desperate, ill thought out, foredoomed, tearjerky for those prone to such states.

That fission should require an incision

to complete was not uncommon, the pressure building to a point where excruciation threatened to overwhelm the fissioning party's consciousness. In these cases, a hernia-like eruption continued to grow and stretch the skin – often between the liver and the stomach, or a little lower, between the stomach and the transverse colon – until a cut was made and the skin ruptured to allow the swelling to reveal itself. And that which spilled out, unfurling like a slow-motion jack in the box, invariably looked like what might be best described as an acutely dehydrated human being, an all but evaporated lifeform, a body in such an extreme state of efflorescence that it could almost be a food stuff made from the entirety of some unfortunate creature, some desiccated being that then quickly took on its anticipated arrangement, as if rehydrated by every available drop of moisture in the air.

Although organs were frequently expressed beyond the skin momentarily (sections of small intestine, spleens, bladders, etc.), they were rarely if ever damaged during the process and could be pressed back into place with the fingers, effecting no lasting damage. Dislocations and bone fractures were, however, more prevalent; and while this orthopaedic risk should not be overplayed, fatalities were not unheard of. Only once had he seen someone's spine shatter as a direct consequence of fission. The man in this instance died almost at once, and did not appear to suffer in the preliminary stages, as he'd come to expect. But mostly, when it happened, it was just a rib that went, or a sternum, or a clavicle, possibly a cracked pubis. Where they arrived as if vomited, a dislocated jaw was the primary osteopathic concern.

He could still remember the sense of anxious wonder he'd felt on first seeing a multiplication take place. The comments section, which he'd read before viewing, was close to unanimous in its condemnation of the footage as a hoax, and yet only a few seconds in he somehow knew it wasn't, and that he was watching a new kind of truth emerge, a truth that would continue to emerge far beyond the world's facility to recognize or accept it. The armpits of his shirt were saturated by the end, and what negligible breeze was afforded in his study that late afternoon became apparent there and in the minutes that followed down his back and over the tightened surface of his face.

The Banganga Tank was incapable of

healing all the people that were drowning in it. More arrived at all times of the day and night, but there was less and less water to go round and more dead bodies than the water could heal. The once clear and holy liquid, now surfaced with a scum of human waste, darkened daily on its faithful, who dreamed of maybe one day following the water back to the Ganges and being cured there from how many they would become. On the pole rising up from its middle sat a macaque with its eyes gouged out screaming at the sky.

Kaal felt himself eating for two again.

He couldn't stop. He felt the nutrients haemorrhaging off somewhere else, to some part of his body to which his awareness did not even feign access. He felt something else growing inside him, some recrement refusing to leave, a source of continued pressure inside his head. He tried starving himself, but he soon gave up and ate what his body wanted whenever it wanted it. He awaited the mutilation of his body like a death sentence insufficient to the task. It was only during these bouts of extreme hunger that he concerned himself with the prospect of his running out of food.

There were other rooms, utility closets and the like, full of food and water, stockpiled by his neighbours. The old man had brought them to his attention, told him their rough dimensions and their whereabouts, but he'd no inclination yet to see them. That they could not be larger than they were was about the size of his potential ruin, and salutary. His living space was slowly becoming the size of the death he would exact. As the days and weeks mounted, the rooms around him seemed increasingly pressurized, like the most insignificant breach from outside might obliterate the entire apartment. The pressure matched the one that grew inside his head.

He remembered the white sofas on the

roof of the InterContinental Hotel. He remembered the sea seen from there, Marine Drive's crumbling art deco blocks like a fading advert for itself, for the sanity of being alive. There was a woman sat across from him. She played with her glass on the white table, moving it in slow circles, transcribing a pattern in the moisture from its base onto the recently wiped surface. The people at the other tables were talking, some in English some in Marathi. Kaal and the woman listened without taking notice. They waited to hear themselves speak. The sea was turbid. It was late afternoon.

The Bandra-Worli Sea Link, only its

upended Y-shaped piers still visible, was silhouetted against the glaucous flatness of the horizon, stretched purposeless across a blurred section of the Arabian Sea, now partly reclaimed with drowned bodies reaching all the way back to the shores of Mumbai.

The Phiroze Jeejeebhoy Towers would eventually go under. The encampments on its roofs would be swarmed and dragged down beneath the new ground level. The Rajabai would be next, days later. The sight there now of many corporate types persistently holding their phones to the air, as if to a god who had abandoned them without due notice.

The butlers at the Oberoi had occupied the rooms they'd once been assigned to as mere drudges. They had locked the doors to their respective suites and didn't intend ever coming out. The pictures showed them in various states of enthusiastic habitation: posed, reading in large red armchairs, submerged in deep standalone bathtubs, at desks or on settees that looked out to sea, or else with their feet resting irreverently on the keys of expensive black pianos.

At the Aer, the beautiful set, too conscious it would seem of their singularity's inevitable and continued diminishment, were mixing their own unique and near-lethal brand of cocktail, and throwing themselves off the rooftop. The crowd of Mumbaikars below was yawning enough in its depth that there was no fear of them ever hitting the ground.

The islanders on Elephanta were refusing to allow the ferry to dock. It was repeatedly turned away, each time overloaded and perilously unstable, with gunshots and threats of violence. (The three main landing quays, the Mora, Set, and Raj Bunders, had all been destroyed to make secure docking of larger vessels all but impossible.) Those desperate enough to escape the choke of the mainland, and the near-suicidal bedlam of the Apollo Bunder in particular, jumped overboard and attempted to swim for it. For every one that made it ashore, fifty more drowned in the harbour (mimicking the elephant it lost), or else were shot or forced back onto the ferry. The 1200 inhabitants had already trebled on their own, and there were at least 1000 more interlopers from the mainland, arriving not only on the ferry but smaller private vessels as well. Butcher Island faced a similar daily onslaught; and even though its port authorities were less vigilant than the indigenous Elephantans, its smaller size and inhospitable terrain made it a less desirable sanctuary.

The situation across India was no different, a fact perhaps best conveyed by the dome on the Taj Mahal Palace, its Indo-Saracenic overstyling now once again on fire and all but coated in layers of climbing bodies, the flames and smoke belching into the greyed sky, dwarfing the tower of its new wing – where the roof, yet to be reached by the sprawl outside, showed no sign of movement. Kaal found it hard to take his eyes away from the stillness there, as still as the room around him, both giving the impression as of looking at a memory.

Bloated rats, their bellies full of children's
toes, buried themselves in the dead to rest, the bodies blackened

with insects, crows hopping from face to face pecking at eyes.

Somehow they had found each other, hundreds of bereaved women imploring the sky, the modulation of their voices warping in and out of a single shriek. In the background, volcanoes of bodies belching blood and limbs and perverse noises from its hidden undercurrents. The infinite in the guise of a nocturne, decomposing, leaking pus – the smell of centuries-old carrion in a jar.

When the drone strikes hit they did little more than displace bodies, the explosions throwing them into the air like sprays of spring flowers. Blood in thin jets squirting from all angles. He thought how all blood had become menstrual blood, become a longing for some bygone sterility, when biology knew its place, when apoptosis counted for something.

The last images he saw of the cellular

ceiling at BOM's Terminal 2 building were filmed on a phone from close range. There was what looked like blood dripping off them, and hands pushing at the raised edges trying to keep them away. Others nestled up inside them and prepared to suffocate. There was a resignation to what was going to happen that he didn't understand. He still remembered the white peacock-tailed pillars reproduced on the glass and the floor tiles, a pristine space of light and refracted grandeur. He remembered how empty it was, and how this picture he'd seen was superior to the real thing. And how, although he was pleased to see his parents that day, he was nevertheless back in

India under duress of conscience – his mother's dying – and how the instantaneous evaporation of the postcard image he'd superimposed over the real thing was the first sign that his imagination might no longer be equal to the task of living.

Devout Hindus suffered religious deprivations in addition to those endured by most other people; for their faith, not being a collective experience but a quiet contemplative one, meant that their temples were reserves of solitude rather than likeminded amassment, and the religion itself was poorly tailored to the swarm. For this reason among many, Kaal was glad his mother was already dead.

Of the two clutches on Elephanta Island,

the Hindu caves were by far the more populous, the Buddhist caves (located to the east, on the Stupa Hill) being not only less in number but considerably smaller in size. You couldn't say, then, that Shiva was more of a draw, even though all those extra arms and heads and eyes seemed more apposite to the comforting of multitudes perhaps, as the crowd's many theisms, or variations on their absence, were trumped most every time by self-preservation and personal comfort. Crammed inside the cave of *that which is not* were *those who are too many*. Bodies were packed so tightly against the basalt rock, their fingers hooked up inside the bullet holes, they could almost be reliefs themselves. (And who knows, some free-thinking members of the Archaeological Survey of India might have even approved of this modern, rampantly polytheistic rendering of the Mahādeva.) Small boys were jammed in around the heads of the Trimurti sculpture, their blood-stained trainers swinging to and fro above the central face. At high tide about a third of the island was lost to water, and a good number of the islanders too. The cavernous ravine that once divided the island from north to south was gone, long since filled with humans. As the entire island turned into a wiggling mass of flesh and secretions, Gharapuri on the south was too deep in its populace to be distinguished as a village. All arboreal life was underfoot: the tamarind, mango, karanji and palm trees flattened beneath an amalgam of multiplied residents and mainland exiles with no direction to go but up.

There was no record of who built the caves on Elephanta. But, whether they were constructed by men or by epic heroes, they were there and their dimensions and architectural features had been noted. Kaal recalled how Cave 1, also known as the Great, Main or Shiva Cave, had two entrances, and that the entrance to the north had a thousand steps, how as a child of no more than 11, his parents a few steps ahead, he'd descended them, and how to his right there was a panel depicting Nataraja, while to his left, depicted in a matching panel, was Yogishvara.

All around the walls of the main hall were carved depictions of Shiva, each in excess of 5 metres in height, which included compartments located at its four corners depicting his marriage, his dwelling, and the demons with whom he was in conflict. The Trimurti sculpture, with Ardhanarishvara to its left and Gangadhara to its right, was situated in a cave on the wall to the far-south, directly in line with the entrance. It was 6 metres tall and depicted a three-headed Shiva. The three heads were said to represent creation, protection and destruction, and the flower bud in his hand a promissory object ensuring life and creative force.

Abruptly, there superimposed over the top of his remembered representation of the statue, was Marion Crane moments before she died, stood naked in the shower, her hand held out in front and shaped like a flower, as if watered from above – the same above from which the camera would soon presage her murder. And later Arbogast's too. In her case, the flower's insurance had been an empty one, an inversion of Shiva's, auguring instead death and Norma(n)'s annihilative force. Confounded by the way this image from a half-remembered film had managed to bleed into his reminiscences of childhood, Kaal tried to focus on something else. He sat looking out at the terrace from bedroom 3, saw the decking, the wall, the sky, the glass in between.

There were two much smaller chambers to the east and the west of the Trimurti cave, but he could not remember what he saw there. And, of course, all of what was not hidden then was hidden now – if not by destruction then by the increasingly dense terrine of humans now resident inside it.

Trying to ignore a scratch that had

appeared inexplicably on the coffee table – thin, curvilinear and approximately 10 centimetres long – Kaal trained his eyes on the computer screen and concentrated his attention on not looking away. He watched a live-feed from IIM, Ahmedabad. It was midday and the shadows draped ominously, from right to left, like a Chirico painting. Only there were people scattered everywhere. And in the middle of the screen, surrounded by others, were three men raping a woman. Most of her clothes had been torn off and she looked to be bleeding profusely from the face. The men took turns holding her down and standing between her legs with their trousers round their ankles. At intervals, someone else would approach, strike her with their fists, and then move away. This woman was being defiled and beaten as he watched, and yet the distraction was not enough to keep him from thinking about the mark on the table. He did his best to keep his eyes on the video, but he kept looking away, in the direction of the scratch, consumed by what it meant and how it had arrived there without his noticing. After some interminable period staring at the gouged table, a sickly and almost unworldly note rose above the otherwise febrile hum of the humans at IIM, and he turned back to the screen. The woman in the centre was either dead or unconscious. The men stood around her watching, their trousers still round their ankles, as her intestines started to float out of a gash in her stomach.

Kaal pictured himself back at the Chatterjee

& Lal gallery exchanging glances with a woman as he made ponderous circuits of the room.

The arrangement of the pillars and their capitals had made

him think of pillars in the Shiva cave. Air conditioning units hummed above his head. The walls and ceilings were white, the floor, surfaced in oversized tiles, a marbleized cream. The footsteps of the visitors were discordant, the overall commensurability of pace refusing to synchronize. The show was *A Thousand Kisses Deep* by Fabien Charuau. He remembered there being nine canvasses.

The woman whispered over his shoulder that she thought a thousand was somehow too deep. He wondered if it was anywhere near enough, and thought he remembered whispering back as much. He heard someone say how the title was also the title of a song, by Leonard Cohen, and a poorly-received film involving time-travel. On the canvasses were digital prints, some luridly coloured, some much less so, looking etiolated, as if by the picture's own internal glare. Only one was entirely monochrome. All had underlying geometries traced out in thin, mostly straight lines. One pattern resembled a piece of quartz, others a crevasse in a glacier, a splash of water replete with squares and triangles, a range of mountains, an horizon.

The images were once photographs of Indian couples kissing, which Charuau had then processed using an algorithm to determine each pixel's relative vicinal congruity, a pixel's similitude or dissimilitude to its neighbouring pixels creating semi-abstract topographic groupings in broadly crystalline patterns. The colours and sections used in the finished works were chosen by Charuau in an attempt to capture the hidden quintessence of the original images. That these instances of arbitrary togetherness should imply a correlative affection contained within those parts struck Kaal as naïve at the time, and as demonstrably absurd now. There were, however, organized structures revealed in these aggregations and disaggregations of pixels which, in spite of the capricious nature of their arrangement, seemed to disclose a surprising degree of underlying cohesion; and if, as was claimed by Charuau, his intention was to reveal the fundamental physicality of images, then these configurations could just as well be seen in states of near mutual animosity as in near mutual affection, giving us *A Thousand Stabbings Deep* in answer to his *Kisses*.

The body on the terrace, laid out east to
west in front of the plants at the north end of the living/dining section, did not move. Or rather, if it moved, its overall position did not alter. For there might have been some negligible local activity to the skin around the mouth and throat, and about the chest and stomach beneath the shirt it still wore, beneath the black plastic sack over the top of that. He'd so far confirmed no such movements, and certainly no fluctuations suggestive of breathing, for instance. If he thought he saw these changes his self-doubt proved greater than the actual seeing itself. There was the implication, however, that the man's death had not yet been achieved, and that the body, though obviously and emphatically motionless at a glance, still waited for it to arrive.

Scanning the top layer of the deepening

amassment at the base of the Tower revealed increasing numbers of those actively seeking to kill themselves. A dearth of weapons had put fragments of windowpane at a premium, and what looked initially like people desirous of leaving what had been the street for the imagined sanctity of the buildings around which they were clotted, frequently disclosed an altogether gloomier aspect, as the glass was broken and fought over with rapacious vigour and, having been won, rapidly self-administered into necks and thighs and wrists. More prevalent as time went on, these incidents remained less common than he would have predicted. He surmised that the rest, the majority, were still unable to grasp the permanence and eventual worsening of the global situation. There remained, he guessed, something inescapably oneiric about what was happening to them, and as a consequence it was understandable that they should yield to the temptation of imagining an equally dreamlike cessation to it. And given the emphatic rupture of their former epistemological bubble, that this could end just as quickly and as inexplicably as it had started wasn't really such an unreasonable conclusion after all.

Kaal's fenestral markers depleted week by week, as the horde continued to churn and swell and consume the space between him and the reconstituted ground. Overall upward growth was, though, of less immediate concern than the concentration of activity around the Tower itself. For moulded all around its base was an exponential curve of swarmed humans more than doubling its reach. At the current rate, he figured he had just six more months, perhaps less, before they breached the bottom of the top two levels.

During daylight hours the human swarm

was frequently obscured by another, airborne variety. Thick, smoke-like throngs of houseflies hung above the people on the ground, swooping down in thin swathes, like tentacles from some amorphous cephalopod mindlessly stroking at its victim. The main body of the swarm appeared to play with the sunlight, displacing its heat, swirling and contorting, desiccating then blending, frolicking in undulations, the pitch of the waves seeming both random and coordinated, an intelligent mist absorbed in its own palpitating bacchanalia of effortless synchronicity. As its parts died there were more to replace them, more than there were before, and then more again. The levels of insanitation were beyond these insects, and you could almost see the desperation to keep up, to capitalize on this heaven on earth, this too abundant resource, this world in its entirety transforming into vomit and into shit.

Kaal could not remember ever having

been inside the GMS Grande Palladium, but knew he had seen its ground-floor lobby through glass on many occasions, and was as familiar with its exterior as he was the deteriorating contours of his own middle-aged body.

The building's arrangement at first appeared wilfully chaotic, but like the slums, it was supposed to resemble its composition was persistently deliberate and utilitarian, its aesthetic one of unfettered practicability. It had been thought by some to look like a spaceship that had landed between the corporate complexes of the business district and the Dharavi slums, assimilating the architectural features of both, and thereby offering itself as an antidote to the Bandra Kurla's sterile, glass-laden monoliths; and so although the GMS may have appropriated its contours from the surrounding area, either in sympathy or opposition, it never stopped looking like it had just landed there, and what's more, could remove itself at any time.

Kaal began visiting the building regularly some weeks before the acceleration, and these summations of its purpose struck him as accurate; for what ostentations he observed in its construction were there, he thought, in its jarring appropriations of an imagined future, rather than in any fatuous attempt to achieve some timeless evocation of grandeur.

Aside from the two basement levels, and a clubhouse that sat alongside it like some errant shuttlecraft, the building's six-storey podium was propped eight metres above the ground on white stilts in the shape of inverted pyramids. It had narrow cantilevers, the most prominent being the director's tube, which jutted insecurely from the apogee of its west facade. Eschewing any traditional architectural garnish, there were instead faceted and ribbed aluminium planes that deflected the load of the cantilever into the ground – one example among many where the GMS could be seen to wear its structural innovations on the surface, like the exoskeleton of some alien insect.

There were horizontal sun-shaded fenestrae to the west, and large tessellated glass aspects on the east and north-facing walls. The north facade was dominated by a faceted miscellany of triangulated sections of laminated glass, while the south facade, lucifugous in contrast, had only 12 unimposing horizontally orientated fenestrae. A projected roof to the east and west, with only the slightest of overhangs, sat above a horizontal bank of glazed panels. Underneath the podium was a landscaped courtyard and thoroughfare, with an external ramp leading up to the main entrance.

Although he knew that the client and his son occupied GMS's cantilevered tube, and that the remainder of the podium structure was dedicated to office space, he did not ever imagine that he had as a result been conferred its real purpose. For instance, it was not insignificant that the faceted panels on the surface of the GMS deflected the weight of the cantilevers that extended beyond the structure, apparently unsupported. Also, that the GMS had a series of utilitarian lobbies in place of one imposing atrium was of importance, lobbies being spaces of transition rather than arrival. No one view from outside was ever replicated in any of the other available perspectives. It was an amalgamation of seemingly incompossible facades. Its being one thing instead of many was something he never took for granted.

Again, the structural composition of the GMS was not hidden behind aesthetic embellishments, but worn on the surface, ornament and function coalescing in an arrangement that suggested alterity, movement and indeterminacy. What was incondite one moment was a flourish of expansive design the next. A genuine melding of purpose and aesthetics could never lose its impression of being outlandish, for the simple reason that we need our meanings to be useless; and this went some way to accounting for why the GMS appeared to have travelled to Mumbai from another planet, another solar system. Because pleasing arrangements always seek their justifications elsewhere, Kaal thought of the building as a tesseract, as the distorted shadow of some extra-dimensional dwelling that he would never get to see.

Use-value is always sordid, and we cannot be the sort of creature that locates its higher sensibilities in what is innately low. In other words, the GMS revealed to Kaal the dishonesty of every passing minute it refused to deracinate its props and disappear up into the sky.

There arrived millions of humans across

the world who would never see the sun. They would live underneath other humans, amongst the bodies of the dead, burrowing like moles through their compacted layers, surfacing only to create inlets for air, but never venturing onto the surface and never opening their eyes.

In the evenings, the birds regurgitated the half-digested flies they'd eaten into the throats of recently hatched birds, themselves already covered in flies. All parts of those buildings still visible, with their once white concrete and glazed facades, turned uniformly black, the patches joining together to form an unbroken veneer. He couldn't see the depth of what coated them, how many layers there were crawling over and into each other, jostling for some optimal yet seemingly endlessly unachievable position to form this density of blackness, and yet he knew this perpetual agitation was there in the detail of it.

As the sun went down the flies moved onto the terrace. They formed a carpet over the floor and the walls, over the seat and over the plants, up the glass and over the body. Like the sun had burnt itself out, solidified into a gargantuan black mass and then shattered, raining its pulverulent remains on the earth like a child's vivid imagining of the night.

There were, by his best estimate, at least three layers of human and other mammals composting beneath at least two more ground level human layers still variously convincing in their attempts at being alive.

The heat came at them from above and below and inside: from the sun and from the decomposing creatures beneath them and from the fevers they'd contracted. The temperature increase was marked and all but impossible to displace, for even the surface lamina had no space for the air to circulate. There was only the scaling of buildings in an attempt to escape, buildings that for the most part did not facilitate straightforward or even plausible ascension, with those that did already proving as congested at the top as they were at the bottom.

The ghost of the human was slimy, bloated and sad, as is anything that dies without actually dying. A monstrous snail feeding off its own decaying parts, secreting blood to lubricate its passage back into the past, into the land of grazing leviathans and beyond, into less recognizably corporeal immortalities and dimensions.

They became their corpses. Only, in order to realize this identity, they first become double, then triple, then quadruple… they become death looking back at itself, a death proliferated like so many faceless, chugging bacteriums, an abundant horror of abundance itself, a birthplace of fractal disincarnations, sad mothers of their own infinite potential to die. Everywhere were birds eating the flies until they were sick.

The frenzy of the crowd had waned

overnight. Its parts moved if at all as if in a desultory and aleatoric trance. Only the new arrivals had the energy to make noise or move with any sense of urgency. They took over the most coveted positions on the roofs, throwing the weak and the sick over the edge with very little effort. A shortage of water meant dehydration was inevitable, and with liquids continuously pouring from both ends, remedying it even in the short term proved almost impossible. Some of their mouths were so exsiccated they looked to be glued shut, while others coughed so much their mouths were never closed. There were also those whose eyes were sealed up in addition to their mouths, a yellowish line of mucoid discharge marking where the eyelids met. Movement was sluggish. They appeared drunk, falling over, reeling and collapsing, trying and failing to get up, shitting out brown water, mucus and blood, vomiting spools of dark liquid in their sleep. The more flies the more diarrhoea the more diarrhoea the more flies: there was no seeming end to this cycle of shit and death that threatened to replicate itself over and over until the moon passed the Roche limit and disintegrated around the Earth to form a ring.

Men stood on the top of the Kanchanjunga Apartments pissing blood over the edge, each red arc splashing back against the pale cut-out walls and resembling streaks of rust. A boy stood beside them wearing only a pair of shorts, they were soiled a reddish brown at the back, and his chest and abdomen were covered in rose-coloured blotches suggestive of typhoid. A woman, perhaps his mother, slowly circled the roof. Her head appeared to be missing the uppermost part of its cranium. He thought he could see her brain. Gradually the area darkened and grew outward with flies, grew into a living, palpitating fright wig. She walked underneath it, oblivious, content almost. He remembered this scene without wanting to, remembered their faces like he'd known them. He never bothered hypothesizing about whether any of them were still alive. The thought didn't even make sense to him anymore.

He recollected a video, from before the acceleration, which could have been an advert for the future. It showed a man wearing his anthrax like it was the ill-fitting skin of some other man. There were sores around his neck and armpits with small black eyes at their centres, and angry, swollen areas elsewhere on his body that he scratched at incessantly. His neck was swollen and he found it hard to breathe and to swallow. When he coughed it was invariably accompanied by a liberal spray of blood. His movements, slow and increasingly measured, were clearly a source of intense pain. A proud Jharkhander, he wouldn't be leaving. There was no risk, no disease that would make him leave his district, the district where he had been born. The interviewer went quiet, the man looked confused, scared even. Blood in the shape of a worm appeared to be lifting off his face.

He felt the jolt in his trapezius as the descending binoculars came to the end of their safety cord. In a split-second, in an extempore reaction to something seen, his hands had opened allowing them to fall. He heard the binoculars collide with the outside of the terrace. He laughed at the degree to which he could still be squeamish. It was funny like it was someone else's absurdity he was glorying in. The faces, mouths open in what looked to be screams, and every visible surface, inside and out, bristling with flies. They looked to be suffering from the worst imaginable case of hypertrichosis: over the eyeballs, the insides of mouths, the humans underneath evoked only through expectation, rare glimpses of skin, and general outline.

He wasn't sure how he'd arrived at it. The page came immediately into view like a pop-up, only he couldn't think what he'd clicked on to instigate it. The film was the user's only upload, and its date corresponded with the first surge of division footage, so that whatever consternation and notoriety was anticipated for it never came about. The first installment of the video had no responses or comments and only 52 views, discounting his own. As he watched the first installment online, the remaining 194 sections (along with some supplementary files), each an hour long, were installing themselves onto the hard drives of every one of his computers, and once there infecting the video software so that no other files could be played. Its title, *195 Days in the PsychoBarn,* seemed to him laden with intrigue, but was also, as it turned out, just as deliciously prosaic.

The artist/filmmaker referred to himself a NB: a deliberate ambiguity used to evoke not only the structure's rightful resident, but the abbreviated Latin instructing us to take special note of what it was he was about to reveal. A few minutes research uncovered that the name behind the initials was Nikolas Berg, a Norwegian artist and recent graduate of The University of Oslo.

The film opened to blackness. The sound of breathing and then words: "Midnight, April 19th, 2016, and the vultures have gone." Over the next few minutes, the voice's surroundings were gradually revealed, the light improving so slowly from one moment to the next as to be almost imperceptible, offering at full illumination, such as it was, nothing more imposing than a close-up section of 3 intersecting scaffold poles, each length a uniform, untarnished silver.

Quite why Kaal was so intent on watching the first installment there and then in its entirety, so anxious at the thought that his connection might go down for good, as it must any day, before he'd managed to see it, was not available to him at this time. But it somehow struck him as being on a continuum with the obscurely purposeful compulsions that had resulted in his taking up residence in the Tower, and that both had implications beyond his desires.

While NB's infiltration of the PsychoBarn

was not visually documented, he recounted it in some detail. And it was at this point that Kaal learnt of his accomplice, Maeva Christensen, who was instrumental in the project's success from beginning to end: it was her who caused the diversion which allowed NB to enter the installation unseen, and would also be responsible for bringing food and water every third day for the duration of the work, conveying any pertinent information (on security, etc.) in notes slipped inside the privet hedge that ran around the edge of the Met roof, and who, as the plan went, would distract the security guards at its conclusion to allow him to vacate the installation and enter the lift unnoticed.

There was, then, no footage of NB and MC entering The Metropolitan Museum of Art on Fifth Avenue on April 19th 2016, of them walking up the steps and into The Great Hall, past the merchandise outlets on either side and straight through and up more steps into the space dedicated to medieval and Byzantine art, of them exiting to their left into the main galleries of European Culture and Decorative Arts, continuing on that same trajectory to the far wall and joining a queue for the elevator, of them finally entering the elevator and taking it up to the fifth floor, or of them exiting there and parting company, NB approaching the PsychoBarn while MC hung back, preparing for her diversionary tactic, in which she will fake an epileptic fit of such terrifying and clamorous magnitude as to draw the attention of every person on the roof, and of NB then slipping round the back of the PsychoBarn, concealing himself among scaffold poles and the huge black water-filled barrels used to hold the structure down, taking the black tarp out of his bag and unfolding it over his head and the rest of his crouched form, the view from behind which forms the first few minutes of the video, initiated hours later, when the crowds are gone and the Barn is swathed in darkness.

Although he rarely slept more than a few

hours each night, the time between the public leaving (4.30pm Sunday-Thursday and 8.15pm on Fridays and Saturdays) and them arriving again (at 11.00am) seemed to shorten. The title, PsychoBarn, as NB pointed out, was most apt during the day, when all other sound was supplemented by the scratching of passing feet and the endlessly layered clucking of the multitude outside.

In these early stages, NB found himself obsessing about weather, wondering what level of inclemency would warrant the closure of the exhibit. He figured torrential rain and/or high winds would suffice, and then he'd be alone for the day, just the sound of city streets and the birds and the rain falling and the wind forcing itself between objects. But there would also be moments when he'd panic about this same risk, and how it would prevent MC from leaving the food and water he needed to continue.

The back of the PsychoBarn faced south-

west, which meant NB got the sun from around noon till late into the evening, while being shaded all morning, at a time when the crowds were yet to arrive and he'd be best placed to enjoy it. After a week of suffering this unwelcome occlusion of warmth and light, he crawled round the edge of the left facade, between the gap in its illusory dogleg, and sat there on the marbled tiles till around 10.00am, when his nervousness at being discovered would get the better of him and he'd retreat back into the maze of pipes and water barrels. When he thought back on those early weeks, the importance he'd attributed to sunlight struck him as diversionary and weak-minded.

When NB panned the camera across the

Manhattan Skyline he did so with no sense of familiarity or attachment, no lingering on any favoured silhouette, no inadvertent pauses as he indulged a memory of some former event or acquaintance. Just a survey each time, from left to right, to capture what was there at that particular instant, with all hours of the day and night accounted for. Same with the trees of Central Park, scanned as if their meaning was the same to everyone, with no one tree or orientation or landmark being any more or less significant than the next. Even The Empire State Building failed to distinguish itself enough to prevent him repeatedly cutting off its apex without so much as a judder. The skyline's refulgence at night too, though multiform and variously coloured and otherwise imposing under the darkened sky, was just so many buildings lit up with just so many lights. But then NB's mission was not to replicate a commonplace touristic swooning, but to occupy a copy of a copy of a copy (Parker via Hitchcock via Hopper – with the somewhat less iconic Plainfield farmhouse lurking in the background like a ghoul) and he was stuck on allowing nothing to distract him from this predicament, from the shrunken manifestation of a fetishized psychosis in which he was not only resident but now somehow responsible for deciphering. And he knew already that explaining would not be enough, and that it was more incumbent on him to embody this simulative lineage than it was to furnish it with ever more pointless detail and comparison.

In architectural terms, *Transitional Object*:

(PsychoBarn) was not obviously transitional, yet with its living space a web of scaffold poles, and its exterior exuding an unnerving combination of gothic horror and bucolic charm, you could easily make an argument for this Second Empire stage set's timeless modernity. However, it was in its

conceptualization that the transitional heft of PsychoBarn was felt most strongly, for in this simulant reconfiguration of a still-contemporary nightmare – one so often reimagined (from Douglas Gordon's 24-hour version to Gus Van Sant's faithful, near frame-for-frame, reworking) that its legacy had itself become as involuted and resilient as the reified human darkness at its centre – Kaal, as NB's adoptive cohort, would soon discover myriad passageways and "opportunities for as yet neglected motilities and points of cognitive egress," as NB put it.

NB repeatedly claimed that what he was performing was nothing more than an "exercise in deliberateness." And he did not expand on this, not right away at least. He left it hanging, like it had dawned on him each time only moments before it was said, almost as if the statement contradicted itself through its own spontaneity.

He had, he said, considered going to Los Angeles and hiding in the real Clatworthy and Hurley *Psycho* house, which again wasn't a real house but only two facades, a stage set to be seen only from a certain angle; but he'd concluded that Hitchcock's version would be too close to the real to evidence the reality he was after. The place he required had to be at least one more stage removed than that, one more step back from the world's supposed concretion, one more step back towards the cliff edge he imagined was waiting there behind him.

NB recounted his first sighting of the

PsychoBarn, how its reconfigured red 1920s barn wood sidings, coloured using animal blood and linseed oil, were faded and blotched, recalled its white window frames and porch posts, balustrades, railings and spandrels, and how the posts here and there were scraped all the way back to the wood in rectilinear sections recalling a previous agricultural utility, how its roof, made from recently imbricated corrugated steel roofing, was both tarnished and new, tarnished in its newness… and it was then he realized, he said, that this would be his life's work, his life's work in 195 days, a life's work he would survive only in terms of its medical definition. He would leave this place a shell, a facade propped up from behind by the fact of his being born and weighted down by the life to which he'd return and which his time spent in the house would threaten every moment to demolish, to upend, to transport somewhere else that wasn't really anywhere at all.

That Cornelia Parker's version of the Bates

residence had been rebuilt at two-thirds the scale of Hitchcock's (standing at around 9 metres tall) was not insignificant. Nor was it merely the culmination of spatial restrictions, its having to fit on the Met roof while leaving enough room for visitors. This deliberately reduced size should also not be too closely equated with consolidating its status as a fake object, positioned somewhere on a lineal narrative of similarly faked objects: it does not say this is a fake house, so much as this is the shrinking possibility of fakery (which is symptomatic, of course, of its interminable expansion).

Each man multiplied like bread, like fish,

each man becoming food for himself, creating hunger in order to sate it, creating hungers for which satiation was unthinkable. This crazed pluralization of the physiological and the psychological devoured all but the most rudimentary foundations of difference. Man's ancient divisions (of flesh and spirit, body and consciousness) became fractal through this forced multiplication. The univocity of the one-made-many did not result in brotherhood, but instead a heightened pessimism turned to its natural target, to existence itself, in ever more aggressive ways – the target of its interests being suddenly so profuse and invulnerable to depletion.

Every third night, at least one hour after

the visitors had made their way back down the elevator, NB went foraging for the food MC had left earlier that day. She deposited the items where and when the opportunity presented itself: when she was covered by an enthralled crowd, or else felt no one was watching. Inside the privet hedge, as close as possible to the house on either side, was her favoured location, offering immediate and readily accessible cover for small and slightly bulkier parcels alike. In the initial weeks he'd found the food hunt irksome, but he soon came to enjoy it, and even began meticulously marking the many different placements onto his floor plan. As he searched for his supplies he came to feel like the animals in zoos, for whom food was not only necessary sustenance but also a welcome distraction from confinement.

The strategy was for MC to each time disguise her appearance so as to distinguish her as much as possible from the last time she had visited. Cheap wigs of various lengths and colours were stockpiled in preparation. The various outfits needed were to be purchased by MC on the days between drop-offs.

What food she would leave had been decided in advance, chosen for its nutritive value and resistance to perishing in hot weather. The liquid left was always water. The fruits were invariably apples, and (pre-peeled) oranges and bananas. There were pulses and mixed nuts. Hard cheese too could be relied on, usually cheddar or an aged gouda. He had a six-inch lock knife to cut the cheese and the apples and anything else that might possibly require cutting. Every few weeks the package would also include a freshly charged battery for his video camera, whether it was needed or not.

The food packages would always include communications from MC, short epistolary offerings to help alleviate his isolation. Any communications from him had to be sparingly conveyed using an outmoded mobile phone, chosen above all for its superior battery life. It would be turned on only for the purpose of sending a text and then switched off again immediately it was sent. If he ever called it would signal some procedural emergency.

According to Parker, the titular object of

transition she had in mind was a weaning device, a liminal contrivance intended to break one dependence in favour of another, the latter (less restrictive or injurious) acting like a surrogate for the former until the subject can do without either. The standard examples being the child weaned off the breast by the dummy, or off the mother herself by means of some soft object, and the drug addict, who through using some controlled substance in decreasing doses is gradually freed of his habit. But, according to NB, the house was neither the mother nor the drug – despite the obvious associations with the waspish corpse of Norman Bates's maternal parent, Norma, from whom no weaning could be achieved. (He also noted how Norma, the mummified mother, is a mummy twice over: both preserved and preserving, over-nurtured and over-nurturing.) The main conceptual apparatus at work here was a different kind of re-familiarization, its focus being how we are taken further away from a primary, autochthonic source of comfort (and comfort of source), and how the PsychoBarn is an instrument of that distancing: ourselves from the real, ourselves from the need for a real. The eeriness, isolation, and (in Hitchcock's case) horrific contents of the source materials, had come to embody only a cosy familiarity. Any disquiet or terror that was once replete in those earlier versions was now gone, having been reduced to diversionary commonplaces, safe memories, and objectified emotions.

The distancing here is not straightforwardly a distancing from some real source, but from the illusion of the real (our human real with its substantive norms and categories), away from the figment of the real and towards the real of reality's disintegration, the real of the world without us, at the brink of which our meanings disperse and orbit our unknowing, where meaning in its most objective sense comes to resemble nothing more so than it does its opposite.

Parker had made an object she did not

understand, and why else, as a serious artist, would she have made anything. She had reasons for why it might exist, its lineage and so on, but these did not equate to her comprehending exactly what it was. She made it because while she could find reasons for its existing, she could not find an explanation in those reasons. The task NB had set himself was to understand the PsychoBarn despite those reasons, to exist inside it on the terms he found there – and not the terms parasitic on it or indeed parasitic on his being there.

From the virtual dark – nothing but the faint glow of the Manhattan skyline to the left of the screen and the tempered lustre of a scaffold pole at an angle through its middle – comes the sound of NB defecating into a bag: the unmistakable susurration of medium duty polythene, NB's laboured breathing, and the eventual wet slump of his latest excretion into earlier examples of equally loosely formed materials.

It was morning, about a week or so in.

NB scratched at the growth on his face in the usual methodical way. The sequence typically ended with him pressing the palm of his right hand over his eyes and holding it there for at least a minute. When he took the hand away this time his eyes were open but unfocused. The camera was in front of him to the right, so that whatever was eventually seen was encountered by Kaal only through the musculature and organs of NB's face. And it was as if something had been seen, something not normally seen there or seen at all. The concentration in his eyes appeared strenuous to the point of being painful. His mouth slowly dropped open, and having fallen as far as it would go snapped shut again, and the process repeated.

NB read from his notes: "This quintessential

haunted house – thrice removed from source, scaled down, deficient two external walls, a roof, an interior – is the material transpiration of a spell, an invocation to some spectral parvenu, an as yet unused revenant engendered not by some single displacement but a glut of them. This ghost is PsychoBarn's true transitional object; and while it will not be immediately recognizable as a ghost (for this apparition may not even be visible), it will nevertheless come to be recognized as the fastigium of abnormality to which every ghost before it had aspired and failed – failing because we saw them only as dematerialized versions of ourselves and not the unworldly children of spaces we ourselves had been so instrumental in unworlding." As Kaal understood it, it was NB's project to unearth this unearthly presence, or rather to bring the earth to it in some experiential capacity, so that something resembling contact might be thought or felt or otherwise known to have occurred. Bates' own attempt to realize the ghost – in the form of his mother, in the form of her homicidal jealousy – had amounted to the haunting of a house reformed into the shape of a man, the human body acting as a receptacle of the unfulfilled longings of the dead. NB planned to reverse this process: he did not want to contain ghosts, he wanted to let them out.

The wood of the PsychoBarn was real,

and NB repeatedly grazed himself on it. In the early weeks, those nicks and scratches induced a level of repose that the otherwise smooth and abstracted features of his environment looked to suck out of him at every turn. It was reassuring how the house clawed at him this way, like they shared a space outside the existential defilement of what he took to be space in general. When he'd hit his head on the scaffold poles, an event of such monotony it barely registered as the interaction of interdependent objects, there was no such reassurance, only the dull pain of a mutually contrived and so far unsympathetic coexistence of performative equals. Where his skin harboured a splinter, its red colouring scarcely less apparent for being subcutaneous, no effort was made to remove it.

Each of the visitors to the Met roof

imagined themselves different from each of the other visitors. They imagined they weren't the same person as the person in front of them, to either side, to their rear, or the same as whoever had occupied the spot on which they were standing before they had arrived there. This was all fair assumption, and they were right, of course. But then the correctness was a superficial one. For he heard them day after day repeating the same stock phrases, the same theories on what the work meant, where the materials came from, those responsible for the salvage and reconstruction, all the usual adjectives employed to convey a personal response that only served to assimilate it with thousands of other likeminded personal responses:

"The wood comes from an old barn in upstate New York."

"Norman Bates never found a transitional object: instead he preserved his mother's corpse and became haunted by her."

"This is a scaled-down version of Hitchcock's *Psycho* house, which itself was modelled on a painting by Edward Hopper."

"Its incongruity with the metal and glass and neon of the Manhattan skyline is significant, an architectural transition replacing a psychological one that never completed, like the structure itself which is deliberately incomplete."

"You can still visit the original version as part of a tour at Universal Studios."

"A transitional object is designed to facilitate the formation of a sense of identity that is independent from some other, more elementary being or habit or object, and this house fails like Norman Bates failed: it vacillates between identities and finds its identity in the vacillation."

"The house fluctuates between reality and fiction, occupying a kind of superposition that never settles one way or the other: it is a home that is itself denied a home."

"This cognitive dissonance is also present in the wholesomeness of the materials when compared to the malignity of the structure."

"Its identity is its lack of one."

"It's California Gothic or Gingerbread, a Victorian Tudor mansion via New England, via Phoenix, via Hollywood, via Schoharie, New York."

"Hopper's house was a symbol of coldness and isolation: standing alone beside a railroad track that promises the proximity of people only at a glance, where the sunlight never penetrates the house but instead creates only an increased depth of shadow."

"The wood is stained with animal blood."

"It's blood and linseed oil."

"Menstrual blood represents the impossibility of birth or original creation…"

Variations on these observations and more are made over and over, and he listened again and again, and sometimes the voice sounded, to Kaal, like NB's own voice, hushed to give the impression of coming from a distance approximate to that of the crowd, but still sounding more hushed than distant, more like him trying not to sound like himself than someone else not having to try.

NB urinated into a 2-litre collapsible bottle,

which he emptied over the edge at various points around the roof garden when the crowds had dispersed. It would have been easier to just pour the liquid into the hedge, but without the necessary fluid to dilute its acids the plants would yellow and die and draw unwanted attention. There was no need for him to plan in advance for the quantities he would produce, other than the volume of the vessel he would need to avoid reaching capacity during those times when he wasn't in a position to dispose of it.

The containment and removal of fecal waste was a far more exigent concern. They had calculated how much waste NB would produce in a day, how much per month, and how much for the full 195 days, should he last that long. Going by weight, he'd produce approximately 0.5 kilograms a day, 15 kilograms a month, and 90 kilograms for the full tenure. But the weight of his waste was not the concern; what they wanted was the volume. The simplest way of converting it was to litres which, using the approximate density of water, again came out at 0.5 per day, 15 litres a month and 90 litres for the full 195 days. In cubic centimetres this worked out at 500 cm3 per day, 15,000 cm3 a month and 90,000 cm3 in total. The conclusion they arrived at was even more rudimentary than the calculations (which didn't even warrant being written down) that led them to it: he would have to crap into bags and throw them off the roof. Their initial insouciance though was short-lived, for if he disposed of one bag a week in a westerly direction, as planned, clearing the roof above the Modern and Contemporary Art gallery below, and the bag hit someone, not only would that person be injured, but the continuation of the entire project would be threatened. Eventually, it was settled that he should use poop caddies, designed for the easy retrieval of dog mess, and throw them as far as was possible in the optimum direction, either every day or every two days, depending on volume. This way the distance achieved would be optimized, the threat to others vastly diminished, and the offending bags most likely mistaken for those of an irresponsible dog owner.

As agreed, NB threw the bags in the same direction each time: south-westerly towards the 79th Street Transverse, a target he couldn't see and had no hope of reaching, all of which was immaterial as his actual objective was a copse of trees just past the edge of the roof on the west side, down past the far end of the Patron's Lounge one floor below. The ideal throwing weight, which regularly achieved the desired elevation and aerial momentum, was exactly two days' worth.

More so than those relating to prandial content and logistics, NB recalled how it was these assiduous deliberations about the proposed disposal of his shit had threatened his aesthetic resolve. He saw his theoretical edifice gradually submerged in a rising tide of bodily waste. The only way he could rid himself of these gathering turpitudes was to anticipate the work as an intrinsically ascetic endeavour, and one in which fasting would be requisite.

NB and MC's concerns about the presence

of security cameras, hitherto vague, were vindicated by an

article they came across in The New York Times. It was dated Feb. 13, 2001, and reported an incident from the day before, in which a 23-year-old man had fallen to his death while performing routine maintenance on the Met's air-conditioning system. The article mentioned how videotape from security cameras had shown the man going about his inspection and the fatal accident that resulted in the man falling 100 feet into a courtyard below. It was also noted that these inspections took place at weekly intervals, and that they were performed when the museum was shut.

The presence of the cameras and the regular maintenance visits concerned NB far more than it did MC. There would be blind-spots, they just had to work out where they were and make use of them, that was all. And as for the threat of maintenance workers, he'd just have to remain vigilant, which was a necessity throughout at any event. NB remained unconvinced that there'd be enough blind-spots to allow him to retrieve his food or dispose of his waste without being seen. Eventually, MC managed to persuade him that the cameras were not manned and that the tapes would only be checked on the occasion of something out of the ordinary happening. For her, nothing had changed: he just had to keep quiet and out of sight as much as possible, and nobody would notice a thing.

As if aware that he'd become prone to somnambulistic idiosyncrasies of some kind, he left the camera running to record himself while he slept. If it weren't for the inexplicable behaviour exhibited in these hours, Kaal might have stuck with his original assumption that NB was paying sly homage to Warhol, while also conceding how this latest foray into the dynamics of duplication had no particular claim to originality. And although the footage could still be thought to endorse these points, what Kaal witnessed could not plausibly be seen as part of some theoretic contrivance. For what happened in these sections of the documentary went too far beyond what was needed to make such a straightforward point, both with regards to duration and intensity of impact. And even if Kaal imagined that aesthetical considerations were indeed the germ behind NB's decision to leave the camera running as he slept, where it finished up served instead to emphatically dismantle any such bearing. If the possibility of art was instrumental at the beginning, then by the end of that first night's recording there no longer remained any question of a solution being reached that wasn't itself a categorical rejection of this possibility in favour of its opposite, whereby any determinate possibility of art became the determinacy of art's impossibility. The project was over at this juncture, which Kaal suspected was NB's objective from the start (the discovery of a breaking point), but over in a way in which it must nevertheless continue: an art freed of being art while at the same time abandoned by all that is humanly real: the manifest alterity, the inviolably alien.

When the sun was at its highest, and

Kaal's eyes, unaccustomed to the glare, were inadequate to the task of differentiating objects, it was as if the tide had come all the way in, up over all but the tip of the Nehru Centre, across the racecourse, flooding the Delisle Road, engulfing Mill Lands, South and Central Mumbai, and beyond the extremities of his vision into and over Bandra, Juhu, Andheri, and all the way back to Thane, Navi, Kalyan... submerging the entire subcontinent. And he seemed to see waves form and break into the sides of buildings, churning swells around the bases of residential blocks halved in size by the otherwise imperceptible depth of the torrent. As part of the same dazzled impairment, he saw what appeared to be calmer pockets of the same liquid collected on rooftops and terraces – or else of something not associated with the encroachment of the sea, but instead the vestige perhaps of some apocalyptic downpour, the tenebrous clouds of which were still in evidence, hovering at such low altitude as to be mistaken for smog – the only movement there a gentle lapping at the edges and the occasional overflow as a meniscus would break and reform seconds later with a corrective wobble. As his eyes adjusted, their formerly squinted arrangement relaxing with no conscious intervention on his part, as if the light itself had succeeded in coaxing them open, the particulate heterogeneity of the landscape returned in quarantined sections, still clouded slightly at their peripheries, of roughly the same variegated patterns, of struggling figures obscured intermittently by sprays of blood and flies, of an incursive sea, not of water this time but of millions of hard little bodies together emulating a comparative softness.

All the once clearly visible roads and railway lines were now just some memory he had, and though he still knew they were there underneath, obliquely merging and dividing, widening and narrowing, kinetic yet motionless, and could trace a line with his finger along every one of their major routes, they were gone in the same way that the people who populated them were gone, having been replaced by versions of themselves for whom horizontal itineraries were of little or no consequence. He imagined the postures and the faces of those that were left down there, cocooned in their cars, in railway carriages and buses, those that had waited where they were, thinking their journey might one day continue, and who were still there now compacted like soil, like reliquiae.

NB would spend most of the day behind

the water barrels, hidden beneath the black waterproof sheet he'd suspended from two intersecting scaffold poles, so as not to be seen by inquisitive visitors who, not content with the self-proclaimed facades, would peer round the back in their dozens every day. For most it was only a glance, and he could hear them at the dogleg and to the rear of the structure: they approached, they paused, they moved away. Some lingered, but most did not. Most were satisfied with having made sure that they had seen the work in its entirety, and were afterwards consoled or disappointed perhaps that behind this edifice of fakery there was nothing less mundane than an arrangement of conventional building materials. What they did not realize, at least he'd never heard it said, was that behind the facades of the Victorian revival house was not the reality of its erection and subsequent solidity, but another far more penetrating and dangerous facade: the facade of purpose that underpinned the artwork's patent purposelessness. They saw the scaffolding and the weighted barrels and, confident that they'd been adequately sedulous in their assessments, imagined the story had ended, that Parker had revealed her workings, her subservience in the end to basic physics, a subservience that, while referencing Hitchcock's own cinematic contrivance, remained an inescapably practical and concrete evocation of man's manipulation of the physical universe. However, this was not the juncture at which the artwork completed, but was instead the confluence of the public spectacle and the private nightmare. For it was here that the facade of the facade was shrewdly purveyed to those with apposite methods of seeing, those whose sight was so contaminated with thinking that they might be thought to suffer from a kind of acute myopia that was in fact its opposite, or else some combination of both: a blindness of some too concentrated seeing.

NB sat beneath his black plastic sheet

with his knees up under his chin, talking breathlessly in a voice that sounded impaired as if there was something in his mouth, a lollipop perhaps: "…That there should be a facade of the facade seems to imply either that the artifice goes all the way back, or else that there was no artifice to begin with

– aside that is from some initial ur-artifice that deceptively propagated itself in accordance with its one principle device, that of obscuring while being seen to reveal. And given that the world in its truest form is inherently paradoxical, both these implications are equally accurate. If duly prepared, we can reinstate the facade at any given point on the route back towards what is hidden; yet this infinitude of points also substantiates that towards which it is moving, the point at which the hidden permits of no facade, which is not the same as its thereby being revealed, but instead the point when the facade is no longer able to conceal, and so becomes itself an object of full corporeal scrutiny – an endpoint, a facade of a facade, but this time conclusive as opposed to inceptive – at which stage we will have travelled as far as there is to travel, and the glimpse at last made possible…"

The old man, again arriving outside

Kaal's apartment and knocking repeatedly on the door, was suddenly impatient to tell him about the number of people left there on the top two floors, updating the list of occupants mentioned in the note he'd attached to Kaal's door, which rebuking the trend had since been curtailed. He'd met them, he said, and was convinced that, with one possible exception, none were of the new kind. Whether or not they'd split in the past, these were the originals. He was convinced he could tell the difference, but when questioned on it had no readily relatable method of distinguishing them. It was an intuition he had learnt to trust and he expected others to trust it too, and was seemingly oblivious to the possibility that his interlocutors might require something more than his own conviction. To the reply ("Whether they're split or not, what's the difference?") he had only a confounded and aggrieved silence. His response thereafter was to skip any more preliminaries and move headlong into relaying what he'd so far managed to glean from his yet cursory interactions with their neighbours.

On the top residential floor was a Mumbai-born woman in her thirties and her daughter. The American husband was yet to arrive from abroad and, whether dead or many, and despite his wife's unerring faith that a reunion was imminent, would never be returning. According to the old man, the wife was like a child, as reminiscent of one at least as her own child, who rarely spoke and whose habit of staring up at the mother's face, commensurately idiotic and pacific, for reassurance, gave the eerie impression that the woman was a ventriloquist's dummy and the girl, for all her benign stupefaction, was speaking through her.

On his own floor, located just below Kaal's, was a larger family unit, comprising a husband, his wife, their son, the husband's grandmother and the wife's brother. He was uncertain as to the nationality of the wife and her brother, suspecting they might be Russian or else from the Ukraine. He admitted they could even hail from Scandinavia; he would have to ask. The old man's evident distress at not being able to pinpoint the woman and her brother's nationality with any degree of certitude made for a ridiculous spectacle, as if something hung on his being right, as if he had a reputation in this area that he was desperate to uphold. The husband was of Indian heritage, for definite, if not exclusively. The overall impression was he thought them dangerous, without offering any sort of justification as to why. Again, nationality was at issue in determining this for certain, so he'd have to suspend judgement until this vital piece of information could be gleaned.

"My mother was Indian, from Kolkata, my father British – if it helps," said Kaal.

"I knew that. An easy one for me. My wife was from the other side, Talcher, but I know Calcutta well."

Wanting to expand on his premonition, the old man recounted how the possibly-Russian wife had admitted to having split once already, and how her son too had divided, at least twice. She couldn't say for sure how many versions of her son there were; because while at their other property in Juhu, they'd been separated for 20 or more hours, when she'd collapsed without warning and had remained unconscious till the next day. Her husband couldn't verify either way and neither could her brother. The old man thought that she too might have split again in that time, but hadn't bothered pointing it out. He was also suspicious of the son's authenticity; for while the products were often distinguishable in some way from the person from whom they originated, this was not always the case and the boy had a greenish hue to his skin and did not look well. He paused at this point, remembering why it was he was talking, how he'd been intending to establish the imminent threat they posed.

These divisions were violent events after all, and violence begets violence, and you need only look at what's happening outside, and the new ones aren't known to us, and ... well he didn't like the look in their eyes, and the fact that he couldn't place the accent of the wife and the brother, and the grandmother hadn't said a word the whole time, just sitting there at the end of the table, staring like there was something moving on the wall behind him and she could see straight through his head...

They'd promised that if any of them split again they'd immediately throw the products off the terrace, but the old man was not convinced. He couldn't be sure they'd actually carry it out, and that the same could be said for any of them seemed to be of no concern to him. And although his eyes just seconds later made a conspicuous lurch to the left, to a particular location on the main terrace area, to the right end of the room looking out, at the level of the decked floor, in front of the potted plants and so the object lying quite still inside its black plastic bag, he did not remark on what he'd seen.

Kaal suffered the old man because he reminded him that he'd existed amicably enough in the world before this, and that a lot of it had sounded the way he sounded: so silly in its earnestness (and yet so rarely earnest in its silliness), so happy to contract while the universe expanded, and all its overthinking just a convenient means of never having to think at all. But it was something else as well, something involuntary about it, as if on seeing him through the spyhole his thoughts had lagged behind his arm reaching to open the door.

Kaal would stand at the edge of the

terrace at any point along the gradual undulation of its flattened S and look over the side, and every time a majority of the faces he saw were looking in his direction, almost as if they'd been waiting for him to arrive. He looked over and, even through the flies and the haze, he could always see them looking back. The noise they made would intensify. He'd see the faces were the shape of faces that were shouting or else screaming; and if there were words, they were all over each other and so too many all at once to be heard. Their drone was indivisible, offering not even the smallest unit of sense. He might as well have been sticking his head inside a hive and listening for a melody.

Judging by the light and time of year, a

week at least into June, it was approximately 8.30pm when the camera for the first time zoomed into Cleopatra's Needle, panning left and right along the irregularly wooded environs immediately west of East Drive. About 50m north of the centre of the Needle, in a vaguely U-shaped area of grass bounded by trees, the camera stopped on a brunette kicking off her shoes and stooping then to peel away her stockings. Her floral dress came up and over her head and was thrown some distance away in the direction of the trees. The bra was removed and spun in the air before it too followed the trajectory of the dress, the knickers propelled there as if they were an oversized elastic band.

Around her were lines marked on the grass, what looked like a room plan made of rectangles and a circle. Before stepping into the smaller of the two rectangles, which was barely off square, she paused for a few seconds as if she'd seen someone in the distance. The camera zoomed out, but finding nobody else in the vicinity returned to its former ratio just as she bent her knees and effectuated an awkward, somewhat arrhythmic gyration of her hips.

Once inside the second rectangle, her half-spread hands made an obscure signal, motioning in small circles, first right then left. Her eyes squinted and both hands came up in front of her face as if to deflect whatever it was that impaired her ability to see. She remained like that, her body tense and rigid, until eventually her muscles relaxed and her mouth dropped open as if in response to some creeping sedative.

There was a rapid intake of breath from NB as a large figure loomed up behind her, having approached from the west. Stopping at the edge of the smaller rectangle, the interloper stood a foot or so taller than the naked woman and was fat beneath the dated dress; the face, covered in a thick white powder with crudely rouged cheeks and framed by a head scarf, looked to be that of a mad old woman's. In the interloper's right hand was a sizeable kitchen knife.

The naked woman barely had time to turn round, to scream, before the knife's huge blade was plunged directly into her open mouth and out the back of her neck. The next stroke went deep inside her throat and severed her windpipe. Repeated assaults on the neck left it collapsed to one side, attached only by a few shreds of skin and muscle. The limbs were still jerking, as if in permanent spasm, for a whole 6 seconds after the head had come completely off.

After hacking at the body some more, one swipe cutting her left breast in two down the middle, while another opened the stomach where some intestine spilled out, the crazed old woman dropped the knife and retreated to the cover of the trees. What was left of the woman finally buckled and dropped, the head off to the right face up, the arms and legs skewed at unnatural angles.

She complained of pressure inside her

head. It's going to explode, she whispered. It's going to come apart. Her eyeballs reddened, exophthalmic, bulging from her skull like buboes. Her mouth open as far as it would go, retching on words it couldn't deliver, gasping for something other than air. The left eyeball deflated and sliding upwards behind the forehead, the socket gaping, dark, filling with smoke. The smoke drifting away from the face and forming in front of her the shape of another human. The prospect it most resembled was a Victorian parlour trick, a green-screened elaboration on the mythos of ectoplasm.

Same time the following night the camera

focused on what looked to be the exact same brunette who'd been hacked to death the night before. There she was again, jauntily kicking off her shoes and stooping then to peel away her stockings. Her floral dress was again removed over her head and thrown in the direction of the trees. The bra did the same revolutions before following the trajectory of the dress, the knickers too launched after them in the same manner.

Around her were the same lines marked on the grass: two rectangles and a circle. Again she paused, looked in the direction of the Needle, and acted out her inexpert twerk before entering the smaller of the two rectangles.

Once inside, her half-spread hands performed the identical gesticulations as before. Her eyes squinted and she raised both hands up in front of her face as if to protect it from something. Her body was tense until it wasn't, until her mouth dropped open and her muscles disappeared back beneath a thin layer of fat.

There was no abrupt intake of breath, NB this time having anticipated the arrival of the fat old woman and followed her approach from the west. Again the interloper stopped at the edge of the smaller rectangle, and again she was fat beneath the dated dress, the face coated in the same heavy white make-up and framed by a head scarf. In her right hand was a large kitchen knife.

The naked woman's scream was interrupted at the same juncture by the knife going into her mouth. Again the blade went in and out the other side. A concentration of strokes to the neck all but cut off the head, until the violent lurching of the body finished the job and it fell to the ground.

The blade penetrated her body at least ten more times, dividing the left breast down the middle and exposing her innards. The assailant retreated to the trees at the same speed and by the same route. The woman's mutilated body remained standing longer than should have been possible before finally collapsing on top of the discarded knife. The head had fallen in the same place, face up, and the arms and legs were bent in ways that seemed improbable.

Five mornings in a row the woman and her daughter arrived there at his door. He heard them knock, but just sat on the sofa and did not move, just waited for the knocks to be repeated. They'd become more persistent with every visit, staying twice as long each time – soon there wouldn't be time left for anything else. The day before, the old man had moved them on, escorting them back to their apartment before, as he put it, they made nuisances of themselves. His commitment to the social protocols of the everyday was something Kaal found at different times to be both vapid and admirable, and could find no reason on reflection to decide between them.

The U-shaped clearing's being free that second time of all traces of the previous day's events – no crumpled corpse bleeding out, no blood stains, no disturbance to the grass suggestive of a clean-up, nothing – impressed on NB the need to keep the camera running. He'd planned to stay awake all night if necessary, but no such vigil was required;

for it was just minutes before the corpse and the surrounding area was transformed into an eclipsing wash of green stars that no adjustments to the camera would correct. Devices at the scene were zapping from multiple locations, so that wherever he repositioned his camera he could not see round or through it. With no way of infiltrating this green glare, he waited it out. Within a few minutes, the laser lights had gone and so too had the body. But, if they knew he was watching, why only mask the removal of evidence and not the event itself, he wondered. Unless of course they wanted it to be seen, and wanted *him* to see it. It was also possible that they had no knowledge of his whereabouts, or that he was filming from that spot, and that possible onlookers were being zapped from all angles merely as a precaution. The question though remained: why the clean-up and not the event itself? Why, unless the possibility of the murder's being filmed was an integral part of its happening, do the one and not the other? He had the feeling from this moment on of being manipulated, but still he knew there was no way he'd be able to refrain from watching at the same time the next day. That he was only seeing what someone else wanted him to see, that its happening at all relied on his being there watching, and that some crucial aspect of its choreography was being deliberately hidden, were all considerations that while they weighed on him did so without diminishing his desire to see more, to work out the why – even if the why was him or some impenetrable point between him and what he saw.

Kaal imagined the stabbed women standing up behind the green zap, collecting up their gowns and shoes and walking away, that however convincing their deaths had appeared they must have been elaborately staged (using a retractable knife, an elaborate prosthesis and several meticulously concealed blood squibs located at specific locations about the pseudo victim's body), and that only this could account for the disparate levels of secrecy.

He stood at the edge of the terrace, his

head craned over the edge, watching the houseflies perform their daily murmurations. He watched them shift like particulated jellyfish, like the desiccated fingerprints of some pertinaciously anonymous god. They moved as a liquid moves, congregating to form whorls and other transient geometries that suggested mind and mindlessness in equal measure. Billions of punctuation marks migrating from the confines of semantics and syntax, free to explode and contract in endless variations on their own meaninglessness.

All the unfilmed hours NB spent under

his black waterproof sheet waiting for the visitors to vacate the roof were interludes that Kaal felt the need to recreate. He imagined the gaps and, by imagining them, imagined there was some possibility of their being occupied. During the early weeks, though NB had no doubt edited out what he considered to be dead content, excising many of those long muscle-numbing hours spent hiding from crowds and trying to catch up on sleep he'd lost the night before to the dissonance of his expectations and the lights across Manhattan, there'd been more talk, more activity. Now, even when Kaal imagined him sleeping in those early breaches, he imagined it as the precursor of the sleep that was coming: the sleep of NB's parallel life, a body twitching and fading and guttering like it was the dream of itself recalled only in part and intermittently in the moments after waking up.

It was late evening on a weekday and NB

was searching the privet for supplies when a noise from the lift sent him, and the camera, crashing to the floor. By the time the camera had settled into its new position, the lift doors were already opening, and exiting through them was a man in blue coveralls. He was average height and weight, with scruffy balding hair and a few days' growth. With a toolbox in his right hand and a silver and yellow stepladder tucked under his left arm, his progress was slow and measured as he negotiated his way northwards. Ten or so paces out from the lift he turned his head and looked directly into the camera, directly at NB, crouched or prostrate there behind it, and there in his face and in the speedily corrected angle of his head, for the short time these things were visible, was the unmistakable look of someone seeing something they had not expected to see. And yet almost immediately he turned away and continued walking towards the north end of the roof.

Once the man was out of sight, NB got to his feet and

scurried along the wall and back inside the installation. With the camera turned on himself he waited for the man to return, or for others to arrive, or whatever way his imminent eviction was going to play out; for he, like Kaal, felt sure the man had seen him, and that he'd looked immediately away and had not confronted him was no assurance that his presence there would continue to be ignored.

But nothing happened: after twenty minutes or so the man returned to the lift, entered it and left, and nobody else turned up until the next morning, when the roof was open to the public again, and the customary prattle sent NB almost instantly to sleep.

The flies got in everywhere: inside lamina upon lamina of human excreta, in sputa and in shit, in piss and blood, in rotting garbage and rotting people, into open wounds and sores, into nostrils and mouths and eye sockets. The flies reaped and they sowed: the fevers, the diarrhoea, the vomiting, the pathogens. Everything about the fly accelerated in the heat: its movements, its life cycle, its mating behaviour. The days got hotter and hotter and the flies got faster and faster at being more and more of themselves. Flies had been following humans for 6 million years, and now that unwearied parasitism had come of age to spectacular effect.

In the same vaguely U-shaped area of grass

bounded by trees stood a naked woman, blonde this time and slim, shifting her body weight without moving, fingering at her hair nervously. Around her on the ground, marked out in thin white strips of light, was a rectangle, outside of which was a larger less elongated rectangle; the smaller rectangle, more elongated than in the first two instances, ran roughly two-thirds the length of the larger rectangle's two longer sides, its far end close to but not overlapping the outer shape's farthest boundary. In the far right-hand corner was a circle, and in its opposite corner a square. It was unclear where the light was coming from, for while it looked to be projected there was no sign of its source. There was what looked like an item of discarded clothing partly obscuring the circle, and a pair of flat house shoes on the ground to her left.

The camera stayed with her, sharing in the uneasy expectation it found there, its movements increasingly tremulous and jerky, mirroring the variations in her visual field by darting in the corresponding directions, up to the treeline and back again in an erratic sweep so as not to miss anything. This went on for a little over a minute and a half (7 seconds longer), until it happened on an approaching figure: solidly constructed, thick in the neck and chest, calves of no great heft, the gait robotic, toes scuffing occasionally along the grass. The figure was arrayed in a long dress of thin material. The hair was long, dark, drawn back and collected at the nape of the neck. In the right hand was at first a glinting surface, nothing more, the reflective blur of the low sun; but the shape when it arrived was unmistakeable: the all too distinctive outline of a large kitchen knife. With a panicky swoop the camera returned to the woman who, though in the same place as before, was gesticulating more feverishly than before, her feet too twisting with increased agitation, into the ground as if to establish roots, as if to keep her from running. Watching the scene back, it took 32 seconds (of the scene's standardized 45, and of the 160 from the murderer entering the outline till its close, and of the approximate 180 of its entirety) to stab her to death – or if not death a state close enough to death to complete its journey without either viewer registering any further visible change.

Once again, Kaal found himself at the computer screen watching *195 Days...* with no clear recollection of having first gone through the preliminary stages needed to arrive there. He put it down to the inattentiveness formed from habit, how it was the very nature of human automatism to pass over what is not only regular but also mundane. The explanation made sense and he settled on it. But stillthere was the suspicion that he was more absent than usual, and for longer than this account allowed for; and that something else was taking care of the mechanics of his day-to-day living, without his being aware of it until his possible influence was nugatory, was a feeling he could only shake through a concerted stifling of all such introspective tangents.

NB was talking, saying how it was the

evening after the third Central Park stabbing, the modulation of his voice plateaued, conveying the date as well, of June 13th. The time of day some 10 minutes earlier than the last time, the spot where the woman was stood now standing empty. NB's breathing laboured as he complained about the heat and the lack of movement in the air, a physical detail verified in the following seconds by the unbroken inertia of the trees. A bank of cloud, having drifted far enough left to complete its transit across the circular facade of the sun, allowed familiar pockets of dappled light and areas too of fiercer illumination to return, the shadows longer now than before and intersecting here and there where previously they'd been distinct. One of these pockets incorporated the U-shaped setting some 50m north of the centre of Cleopatra's needle, the concreted area surrounding the needle itself, and the smaller grassy sections on the near side of East Drive, all of which were still visible, the zoom function being at this point some way short of maximized.

During the incidents on the 10th, 11th and 12th of June, NB's voice had gone through manifest changes, beginning in the flat monotone that he'd slipped into over the weeks spent alone in the house, and ending up a pitchy, gasping noise overrun with unchecked emotion. It was as if NB had been switched back on after being in temporary stasis, as if the world, seemingly irretrievably lost in all its many versions of itself, had returned to him abruptly in those few minutes in the shape of a naked woman being stabbed to death with a kitchen knife. On this fourth night of watching his voice was once again stale and lifeless, as if he was awaiting nothing more revelatory than the arrival of yet another pedestrian.

NB had been taken in by the world at the first provocation, weeks of work undone. He was finding it difficult to see past this peripeteia, past the ease and speed with which his meticulously constructed absorption had been teased apart. So set back was he by the countervailing forces of the world outside the house that he doubted his ability to continue. The task once Herculean now seemed more like that of Sisyphus, like some autoimmune disease of his reasoning and resolve. And yet the 12th evening of June was followed by the 13th evening of June, and there was still enough formula to his actions to put him at the same place, his camera trained on the same grassed area incompletely bordered by trees.

NB zoomed in as far as possible on the patch of grass where the woman had stood, where there should've been blood stains but weren't. Nor was anything incriminating found when he expanded the radius of his search in the hope of catching spatters or drag marks farther out. The geometrical outlines of light were also nowhere to be seen.

The camera zoomed out, blurring the image momentarily, before the frame settled to include the entire U-shaped area of grass and all but the very outer edges of the arboreal boundary. Back to a close-up of the grass to confirm that nothing had been missed the first time: no obvious signs of blood or the effort taken there to remove it. Until out again, from the west (the top left of Kaal's screen), came a woman with short blonde hair dressed in slippers and a grey silk dressing gown, spotted with small, dark bean-shaped motifs, her left arm held across her stomach holding the fabric together in the absence of a tie, walking slowly and precisely towards the spot on which the camera had seconds ago been concentrated, an area now once again bounded in two rectangles of white light.

There was an obvious resemblance between this woman and the woman killed there the day before. They could credibly be the same woman, if one of the women wasn't already dead. As if aware of the camera, and not wishing her face to be captured front on, she kept her head bowed and turned away to her left as she moved closer to occupying the now familiar patch of grass. She threw what looked like small pieces of paper into the circle on the ground, before releasing her grip on the dressing gown, pulling it off at the shoulders and placing it on the ground to her right, over the same circle. Stepping out of her slippers, she stepped forward into the smaller of the two rectangles. Her skin was pale, with no visible blemishes or scars, her frame and height indistinguishable from that of her predecessor. She began stroking the front of her neck and down the length of her arms, and when she turned in the direction of the camera her hands were already there, each one over the respective half of her face, and did not move elsewhere until the rotation was complete. On cue there was a figure in a dress with a knife. Same broadly masculine gait and build, same matronly hairstyle, same rigid and deliberate purpose to the stride. The knife was the same type if not the same token of that type. The strokes were the same inelastic downward-facing lunges, her deflections too unchanged, her right arm stretching out grabbing at something, finding nothing, the inevitable collapse, half in half out the rectangle, all the same, the punctured body dead or dying on the ground at the end, unaltered to NB's eyes and to Kaal's from what was now this event's previous version and most topical source of reference.

On reviewing the scene, Kaal confirmed

that the times spent on the various stages – of approach, waiting, murder and departure – were exactly the same as in the third instance. And whether or not this precise similarity was the cause, the fourth murder appeared to relieve NB of all the agitation precipitated by the ones that preceded it. If anything, the corrective exceeded itself, leaving him more committed to the Barn project than at any stage since its inception. The world around him was falling into line with his imaginings of it. There was capitulation, collusion even, and he was where he was (and where he wasn't): immersed, fragmenting, consuming and consumed by displacement's accelerated accretion, reality having become like so many layers of acetate without end or beginning, growing as it unravelled, shrinking into a no longer recognizable distance as it re-appropriated the entire humanized universe for its own enlightened purposelessness.

He watched flies dart into open mouths,

crawl up into nostrils, seek to ingratiate themselves past the eyes, between the sclera and the conjunctiva. It was as if the flies, in their abundance, were invested with a sense of collective immortality which superseded any individual fly's instinctual attachment to its own continuance, which it somehow knew now (even more so than before) to be negligible in relation to the irreversible growth of its species: a phenomenon clearly evidenced, it seemed, by their sacrificial intrusions into any available human orifice. For no detriment could come to the fly population's aggregated monstrosity by its shedding these proportionally non-existent spores directly into the airways of every suitably configured host.

NB had, of course, recognized from the beginning what was being recreated on that patch of ground off East Drive. He'd noted the similarities and predicted the outcome from the moment he'd first seen the figure in the dress wielding a kitchen knife approaching the naked woman from the surrounding trees, believing unequivocally that the woman was about to die, would be stabbed repeatedly and then perish from the wounds. And yet it had taken him in. The drama of the scene undiminished in its power to evoke the reality of a sadistic slaying. In fact, its looking to him exactly how such a murder would look, and had looked in the past, reinforced his sense of dread and panic and flailing impotence. There was nothing about its status as a reproduction that allowed him room to thereby dismiss it as anything less than the real thing, the realest thing, with all the inevitability of that reality. The second and fourth murders had managed to divert the impact of the first and third in favour of their duplicative surfeit without thereby undermining it. He'd momentarily lapsed into a standardized narrative sequence, whereby each instance of a pattern reaffirmed that pattern (substantiating both its accuracy and the material grounds for that accuracy); whereas now, with a second and a fourth woman stabbed to death in the U-shaped clearing, he'd disabused himself of these atavistic tendencies and resumed by doing so the project he'd been so close to abandoning just the day before. Now the duplication stood only for itself, and instead of consolidating the pattern consolidated only the infinite proliferation of patterns, thus invalidating the reiterative pre-emption of the real, therein superseding NB's earlier anxieties. The stabbed women (whether the same entity or multiple entities) were no longer an instance of the duplicates becoming increasingly real, but of the real becoming increasingly duplicated.

It was around midday, and hot, and visitors

circulated the roof like pockets of warm air having risen steadily from the galleries below. They were looking round the back of the Barn at their regular rate, where NB remained hidden under his black plastic sheet. The camera was on: NB's face in half silhouette, mouth open as if short of breath, voices from the crowd outside pontificating on the usual topics – plus the occasional variation to give the illusion of change.

A man's voice remarked on Parker's "weird fucking hairdo," noting similarities between her hair and Janet Leigh's in certain scenes in *Psycho*. His interlocutor, also male, pointed out how Parker's hair had been that way for years. Someone else, a woman, slightly bronchial, could be heard complaining about the heat and the price of the coasters for sale in the ground floor gift shop. And apparently there was more than one person of the opinion that the PsychoBarn was built from the exploded parts of a shed Parker had used in an earlier installation, and that the wood salvaged was dyed red using human blood.

A sound at this point as of something hard surrounded by something less hard striking hollow metal, and the sound of cursing muffled yet distinguishably louder than the earlier voices. "Wow! so stark and bloodless – like two-year-old vertigo." The camera jerked to the left, removing for between 2 and 3 seconds what little illumination was left after a cloud or something else had passed in front of the sun.

The face around the side of the black plastic sheet was young and bearded and, though dismayed, smiling, the head cleanly shaven. NB's right hand was moving up and down, signalling a demand that the interloper keep quiet. Finding himself off balance, the man stabilized his position by grabbing onto a scaffold pole with both hands.

By late evening every window was coated

in at least one layer of flies. If Kaal wanted to see the moon again, he'd have to risk them getting in, or else go up on the roof, which was also thick with the things, same if not worse than the terrace. As soon as the sun went down all light from outside was gone in minutes. He sat there in the main room watching the specks appear on the glass, watched them walk into and over each other, eliding into larger and larger blots until there was no separating them and only the fluctuating darkness of their amassed undersides remained.

He pictured how they attached themselves to the faces down below, dripping off chins, coagulating around mouths, sliding off in clumps like fake beards. Flies were inside his head when he slept. He tried to get them out with long, thin implements inserted into the ears, the mouth, the nostrils. They crawled out from his head along the implements, up his arms, his neck, and returning to where they'd started re-entered through the orifices there. The cycle continued until he woke. And his arms would ache like it had happened for real; and his head feeling full of flies felt like it had for years, long before the flies were ever like this, before he'd had any good reason to have a head feeling that way.

He dreamt too of eating flies, or rather of eating food that turned into flies inside his mouth, and he'd wake up spitting and gasping for air. He thought of all the dead bodies down there full of maggots, and the ones still alive filling up with them in parts where the skin was broken and the feeling lost, or those parts trapped beneath other bodies, which having already succumbed to decomposition were at best equal parts maggot and human. There were all the flies over the eyes of children and their arms too weak to wipe them away and no mothers left to do it for them; or if left, left themselves too weak or blinded or unfortunately positioned to do anything about it but pray for the expedition of a miracle or of death, while not being sure that they weren't now the same thing. How many versions of her were watching versions of her children, their eyes covered in flies, too weak to wipe them away, wishing themselves cured or saved or dead and not knowing how to tell the difference?

The interloper removed a rucksack from

his back and retrieved a video camera from inside. He pointed it at NB, turning it on with his right thumb. Changing perspectives, Kaal saw NB crouched behind numerous scaffold poles, running horizontally, vertically and at various diagonals, his camera, in turn, pointed back at the man and filming. The screen alternated between the two views, the time between switches decreasing until each viewpoint lasted less than a second before being replaced by the other. Kaal was witnessing NB's turmoil played out in retrospect, the disassociative glitches of someone trying and failing to assimilate hostile external forces, as the watched watches and the watcher is watched and the ensuing conflict offers no mutually agreeable resolution.

Kaal did not need NB's voiceover to tell him that the Barn could not sustain this dynamic, that the intrusion marked a retrogressive step, that the introduction of what amounted to his own copy could only be to the detriment of what it was he was attempting to achieve. At this late stage, it was too crude an example: an additional human presence, the proximity of such a thing, unworking the work with its basic concretizing of identity. As the images of the two men began flashing up on the screen in dizzying relay Kaal already knew all this.

He would see shapes in the aggregated

undersides of the flies covering the exterior of the patio doors. For a moment there would be a human shape, and then another, distinguishable from the previous figure and the one that would soon after replace it.

There were birds eating flies and flies eating birds, and as the weeks went by more of the latter than the former, the flies too copious to escape, too proliferate to ever break from the eating of them, the birds' young impossible to defend: the eggs covered, the hatchlings covered, outside and inside, filling up with smaller eggs, with larvae, with pockets of gases of death. Older birds too heavy with flies to move, to take off, to catch more flies, to do anything but have the flies come to them, to crawl inside their beaks in streams, not as food but as feeders.

The man divulged his name, his nationality.

He gave his profession, his credentials: an artist, had shown in prestigious galleries in New York and LA, had met Gregor Schneider last year in Berlin where the possibility of a curatorial collaboration, focusing on the art of curious habitation, had been broached but ultimately left open, knew Bachelard's *The Poetics of Space* by heart, quoted from it from memory: "the only houses that are capable of possessing individuality are real ones."

NB was silent, couldn't bring himself to acknowledge the reality of the man whispering in his ear, up under his black plastic sheet, whose deodorant he could smell, whose legs and shoes he could see next to his own, whose breath felt warm on the side of his face even on a day like that one, during which he'd sweated away, without noticing, all need to urinate. His tone irascible and dismissive, NB finally ended his silence by quoting Bachelard back at him: "I will be an inhabitant of the world, in spite of the world."

As the last of the day's visitors left the vicinity of the exhibit for the elevator, the man started yanking items from his substantial army-issue rucksack in earnest. There were copious silver plastic packets, tubular in form, which he referred to as "space food," and which he was confident would keep him going for weeks or even months. He also had at least three different methods of recycling his urine, comprising a number of small vials of water purification tablets, materials to construct a solar still, and a homemade charcoal filtration device. The man was so content to talk, to explain himself and his tactics for surviving in the "playhouse" (said in a throwaway tone possibly designed to rankle), and to quote again and again from *The Poetics of Space* ("An entire past comes to dwell in a new house"), that he seemed not to have registered NB's reluctance to speak or engage with him in any way.

A tall woman, who must have lost a considerable amount of weight judging by the excess skin drooling from her arms and over her knees, was stood softening on the rooftop of one of the larger lower level blocks that ran along the edge of the railway sidings when a bird flew into her face and got stuck there. The poor, stricken animal's wings kept beating, beating faster even, as if it might be possible to fly straight through. By the time she got it out, the front of her head was like something imploded, like a casaba melon caved in or eaten away at by a small cadre of rats. Once it was in her hands and away from her face, its flimsy skeleton all crunched up to almost nothing, she immediately put in back there as if to eat it, but the top of her mouth had been destroyed, the cleft and tongue macerated into some amorphous clump, so she just stood there confused, with baggy arms and legs and a now much more insignificant bird, completely dead, and yet held with such considerable force there was still the threat, it seemed, of its eventually flying away.

It was dusk, and the view out over Cen-tral Park was different from earlier examples, the elevation increased by about a metre. The camera panned right into the scaffold-framed body of the PsychoBarn's interior, where NB was sitting on top of one of the water barrels at the rear end of the structure, his breathing heavy, the second artist down below making adjustments to his telescopic tripod.

"You need to see this," said NB, and the man stopped what he was doing, looked up, and started to climb towards him without pause or reply. NB told him where to sit and he sat, his back now to a second camera, elevated some two more metres, towards which he would turn his head every few seconds as if to elicit further instructions. "Down there," said NB, pointing to the U-shaped clearing north of Cleopatra's Needle.

The sun is in the wrong place, thought Kaal, it's too early for anything to happen there. NB adjusted the second camera so it showed just the two of them and the Manhattan skyline in the distance. But there had been no mistake; NB knew it was the wrong time.

The interloper was still watching the display on the first camera, turning it fractionally left and right in the vicinity of the U-shaped clearing. "What am I looking for exactly?" he asked. And he's told to wait. Only 10 frames per second now. The staggered raising of NB's right arm above his head, his bicep and forearm at 90 degrees, the clenched hand's lurching descent onto the nape of the interloper's neck, the blade protruding from the bottom of the fist disappearing inside the base of the man's neck. Returning to 22 frames per second, the hand wrestling to retrieve the knife from its target, the head attempting to turn, the man struggling to get up, slipping on the uneven surface of the water barrels, the blade out and back inside the neck again, slightly to the left this time, the man tilting forward, the blade out, horizontal and discoloured, a spray of blood, rehoused immediately lower down between the shoulder blades, the man's arms and legs desperately trying to achieve purchase, failing, the blade in and out again in and around the spine, the neck, ten more times and the body not moving, NB repeating the phrase "between the house and the non-house it is easy to establish all sorts of contradictions" over and over until his breath deserts him and he's left gasping for air.

NB sat stroking the man's head, wiping the perspiration off his face, watching his stillness, marvelling at it, almost disbelieving the emphatic absence of life he finds there. When he looked back into the camera, his right hand in his lap still gripping the knife, his left hand flat on the water barrel reinforcing his position, he did not appear to be looking directly back at the viewer, but at something behind the viewer, something much farther back that was also much farther forward (backwards in space and forwards in time), looking through him, through Kaal, like he wasn't even there.

During the small window of softening,

a tell-tale prelude to imminent division, the bite of an appetitive adult could take the arm off a child. But if the timing was wrong, the bones insufficiently pappy, the adult would break their teeth and the arm would stay where it was. The predators, though, could usually recognize when their victims were safe to bite without restraint, when the faces had gone all doughy, when the muscles round the eyes barely kept them in their skulls. Although the young were often the easiest meals, with nothing much of them to stop you once you'd started, they still had to be caught, and at their best were fast and agile and sized in such a way as to utilize points of egress unavailable to any adult; and it wasn't as if the young weren't also hungry, didn't prey on themselves and, in greater numbers, on the larger, older versions of whatever it was they were now that they sourced their nutrients from things with faces just like theirs.

Cleaning up took the rest of the night.

Cutting the lid off the top of one of the water barrels proved awkward, and must've taken an hour or more. It was done in such a way that, barring close inspection, it could be put back in place without anyone noticing. Emptying out enough water to allow for the displacement of the body also proved time-consuming, and even then he misjudged it, slightly flooding the area when it came to inserting the corpse. Fortunately, the next morning was a warm one, and the area was almost dry before the first of the visitors arrived.

As far as that evening's other murder was concerned, the sequence of dispatch was largely unchanged, although the physical build and attire of the protagonists were different. The woman was thinner, her hair shorter, in a pixie cut, the hair of attacker's wig down this time, past the shoulders, and blonde and wavy, the body thicker set and taller. The victim wore kitten heels instead of flats, and her robe was green with a large, silver-coloured floral pattern. The murderer's dress was white with roses on. There were subtle differences in the way she died and in the way the murderer killed her, but on a first viewing they were hard to tell apart. Clouds came and went. The whole thing took 17 seconds longer. There were two clearly defined stab wounds to her back, and her legs at the end were spread in an ungainly way. If he'd been able to get in close enough and at the right angle he'd have seen her eyes momentarily dilate – correcting Hitch's mistake, only to repeat it a few seconds later, when her pupils quite inexplicably contract.

The source had changed from Hitchcock's 1960 original to Gus Van Sant's 1998 remake (thereby bypassing – or so he conjectured, its being virtually unperformable after all, or if performed impossible to distinguish – Martin Arnold's 1 minute Psycho from 1997: a film comprising only a Marion-eye view of the showerhead, first dormant, then dispensing water, then dormant again). NB recognized the shift on first seeing her walking out from the cover of the trees. "We're 38 years on," were his exact words, averred without surprise or any hint of deliberative hesitation – almost as if he might have had some fairly established notion of what was coming next, as if he knew it in the same way he knew that the next night's murder (the 6th scene) would not deviate in any way from the one he'd just witnessed.

When NB uploaded the 195 separate

parts of his documentary artwork he couldn't have known that the criminality of his project, having escalated from trespass to murder, would be completed erased within a couple of days. He must have thought he'd be risking, or rather – with no contingency for escape in place – guaranteeing a jail sentence he wouldn't live to see the end of. The work, Kaal guessed, had taken on such magnitude by the end that such an eventuality didn't even merit a mention. The work had made demands and he had capitulated without question in order that those demands be met. There was no equivocating, no sense that a dilemma had been wrestled with: there was only the work, which everyone would see was reparation enough.

NB was available from 3 different angles

in as many seconds. The concrete where he was standing was in the process of drying, forming archipelagos that were slowly shrinking in the morning sun. He was wearing a pair of black sunglasses not included in the first day's inventory, and a T-shirt, not seen before and also missing from that list, which read: "I 🩶 Elisa Lam."

Some days when he slept he dreamt

nothing but the green zap. He still sensed all the usual oneiric fumblings being played out, the trademark randomizations and inevitabilities coalescing to form that so very fragile diegesis, only, when he woke, the green bursts were there keeping it all together, making it resistant to the logic of waking for hours afterwards, and sometimes half the day had passed before the colours of the world came back to him and the dream finally yielded. Sitting on top of one of the barrels in the early evening, he talked of the Rohmer film, *Le Rayon Vert*, and the novel by Jules Verne after which it was named.

The green ray (or flash), around which the two works

Gary J. Shipley

manoeuvre, is a brief optical curiosity (lasting less than a second) seen on clear horizons either at sunset or sunrise. His own green zap had also occurred on the brink of sunset (the mark of something disappearing), but was instead repeated over and over, making of his eyes a garish wallpaper through which no other colours could be seen. Like those cases of pilots who'd reported seeing serial flashes from their aircraft. The phenomenon was apparently due to the layering of the atmosphere – and this resonated with NB.

He remembered the young woman, Delphine, from the film, railing against the superficialities of romance, and how he'd sympathized with her but often found Rohmer dull and how this example of his work was no exception. But then what were Delphine's issues with intimacy but an everyday version of his own? What was he doing but systematically unpicking his own supposed intimacy with the world around him? The heroes of Verne's novel had been fanatic in their pursuit of the elusive green ray, only to have it revealed to them at the very moment they discover that desired intimacy, not in the horizon but in the person next to them, staring into each other's eyes as the spectacle occurs.

This was why he was alone and must stay alone, why he took residence in the house, and why he could not for the merest instant look away. That it was there in his sleep, then, this green occlusion of flares, he took as a presage of eventual realization, a sign that what might have otherwise been regarded as distractions were not distractions at all, but the very constituents from which the world he sought was made.

Given that his having no means of imag-

ining what its successful completion might look like had itself
been the prime motivation for doing it, the apparent futility
of *195 Days...* was clearly deliberate. And with this in mind,
even its perceived failure might turn out to be a breakthrough
– regardless of whether or not he was able to notice. NB, after
all, was seeking the essence in what had no essence, the real in
the proliferated absence of the real, and awareness where none
was available – the beyond in an infinity of copies.

NB sat rummaging through the contents

of an army kitbag, seen from four different angles in as many
seconds. Behind him, up against the wall of the house were two
other bags and his black plastic sheet folded up in a sequence
of squares. The sun was cutting him down the middle, casting
a short hunched shadow to his right. His hands and arms were
wet all the way up to the elbows. From the bag he pulled an
A4 sheet of photo grade paper, the reverse side of which was
blank. He stared at the paper so long that Kaal noticed how the
shadow of his nose had shortened. NB smiled as if it was the
only expression left to him that didn't involve the gradual but
inexorable implosion of his head – a smile forced to the point
of being a rictus superimposed from outside (by the Barn, by
the play of the light through the scaffold poles, by the barrels)
to prevent anyone seeing what was going on underneath – that
which for whatever reason should never be seen, or else was
not even possible to see.

By the time the paper was turned round for the camera, his hands had begun to shake. He let go of the paper with his left hand so he could use it to steady his right. The page had been printed off from artnet: it showed Parker's 2003 piece *Alter Ego (reflection)*, an "installation of crushed and not-crushed silverware." The image showed white gallery space with strip lights and three pillars, various items of antique silverware (candlesticks, teapots, an ice bucket, a tankard, a jug) suspended from the ceiling above their crushed versions, which were also suspended just above the floor. There were seven pictures on the far wall, one of which was obscured by the foregrounded pillar, while of the rest only the vaguest suggestion of their composition was visible.

For someone whose emotional range had otherwise been consistently narrow, NB's response to the print-out was confusing; for having dropped the sheet of paper to the floor, he reappeared behind the space it had occupied, his head down sobbing into his chest. Kaal might have concluded that NB had never seen this work before, and was overwhelmed by this first encounter, had he not already known from earlier disclosures that he'd visited the exhibition depicted in the image, at Art Bärtschi & Cie in Geneva, Switzerland, on more than one occasion, and what's more had written in excess of 10,000 words on it, in a piece called "On the double as anamorphic distortion, the perpetuation of which will necessarily exceed our ability to optically convert it," in which he referenced either *Alter Ego*, *Thirty Pieces of Silver* or *Breathless* on virtually every one of its 22 pages.

The anamorphic image is one that can only be seen in its

undistorted form if the viewer is either occupying a specific vantage point, or else uses a device (typically mirrored) to reconstitute the image, and sometimes is so configured that both the device and the required angle are needed. From most angles, the crushed forms in Parker's *Alter Ego* could be seen for what they were – flattened versions of the items suspended above them – and only gave the impression of being indiscriminate silver blobs from a limited amount of vantage points. Given this, they were not anamorphic in any strict sense. However, they did play with the idea of anamorphosis by offering both the standardly realized version of the object along with its distorted counterpart, suggesting that you see the one in terms of the other. There was also, then, the evocation of some kind of double life of the image, and in this case the objects of those images too. Quite often the anamorphic image will appear flattened until seen under the right conditions, when the two-dimensional shape gains another dimension.

There were also shadows cast on the floor, which served to reverse the relative distortions of the objects that cast them, with the intact objects casting a distorted, non-representational version of themselves, while the shadows of the crushed items were seemingly undistorted and immediately recognizable as the pre-crushed objects. There was something in all this that did for NB's composure that morning, something there that went on to bend the house and the Met and everything in them out of shape, that turned the *Psycho* murders inside out and reconstituted all the weirdness that had gone before into the purest form of something completely unimaginable.

This sculptural depiction of both realizations of the anamorphic image, one on top of the other (2-dimensional and 3-dimensional, decompressed and inflated), and their respective silhouettes' reversal of this mutually distortive relation, with the flattened objects maintaining their figurative integrity while the unflattened objects did not, all compounded to produce a theoretical understanding of the copy or duplicate or double as not only informationally and dimensionally collapsible, but also simultaneously anomalous re its manifest image. Where he saw it all heading was all these versions at once and everywhere.

The various different camera angles had

exceeded 20 when Kaal suddenly grew tired of counting them, for he knew, it was obvious, that they would eventually reach 78 (one for every set-up) and that the house would make him aware of it without his having to tally each incremental stage. And there he was, consecutively from all the many arranged angles – to the right side of the house by the garden roof wall, the hedge above that, the handrail in front with various items of bloodied clothing draped over it, etc. – NB grinning and completely still, his arms down by his sides, limp to the extent that if the hands weren't there extending beyond the cuffs of his shirt you'd have thought them missing. He stood there like a coda, as if some terminal point had been arrived at, as if the cooled exhaustion in his eyes represented some state outside of himself.

But there were still weeks left, hours of video, and so much too early for perorations of the kind embodied in these increasingly awkward minutes. And the inevitable cut arrived and kept arriving, shifting perspective on the half-second: NB hanging from the scaffold from his armpits, on top of one barrel, and the next and the next, sitting on the first horizontal scaffold pole, the second, the third, leaning up the mansard, up every diagonal pole, on and on until the house was filled with him – a horror vacui begun by the ornamental farrago of the house's Second Empire design and its internal maze of structural reinforcements and completed now by NB's frenzied ubiquity. And yet… and yet an underlying or overlaid emptiness prevailed in all this clutter, a repeated nothingness, an agitated papering over of a void, perverse in its continuing to bleed through, the self-same emptiness present in the indeterminately distant focal points of NB's own exploded gaze.

Kaal dreamt the U-shaped clearing and

in it a slight female with short blonde hair, indistinguishable from the others, stabbing herself to death with a kitchen knife. Sitting opposite her, cross-legged on the grass masturbating, was a thick-set man in a floral dress. Seconds after his right arm stopped moving, the bursts of green light appeared, and there was nothing else.

Between each copy there is always the

possibility of another copy, and a copy too between that additional copy on both its sides, so that the space is never not becoming increasingly full, and the space between copies increasingly small, regardless of the area's containment; and while this would seem to give us a state approaching maximal density, where that density implies the eventual formation of a new single entity devoid of duplicates, we never arrive there and the copies proliferate and the area's infinite emptiness prevails.

Kaal would hear the old man pass his

door, and watching sometimes through the fisheye, see him walking with a festinating gait, his hands turned black, see him dressed ten or more different ways in a single day. If the old man ever knocked, or the mother who still returned there on occasion, he ignored it. If it was possible to forget how to talk, then this had happened, and he did not want to listen. What would they say? To what maturated drivel would he be subjected, the weeks spent isolated in the Tower having turned what was already suppurating into the most queasy-making sludge? He had no more desire to ingratiate himself with his neighbours than he did with the humans outside the Tower. As he'd ascertained already from brief meetings, and from the notes attached to his door, their waking remained bent on solution and their sleeping increasingly fitful or else unclaimed. The solutions they sought were those that would keep them in the Tower, away from the rest, indefinitely –

living, doubling, trebling, etc., but somehow never becoming subject to the squalor that entailed. Whereas he could envisage no practicable means of subduing those outside, or of halting their ascent, nor could he imagine from where a helicopter might arrive, or where it might take them once it got there.

"Copying feeds on itself and once started

can never be finished; and as all moments already exist so too do all copies, and there are perfect copies and less than perfect copies, each again copied regardless of fidelity to their originals, and so the space for original creation shrinks and grows at the same time: to zero on one level and to everything that could ever possibly exist on the other. That not all replication is exact initiates difference not at the expense of sameness but as a fuel for the (qualitative) expansion of sameness, whose remit would otherwise be merely numerical, the endpoint of which is an (ever elusive) state of self-sameness, which then in turn would be susceptible to copying, and so the balance of perpetual incompleteness is maintained. But difference on this model is decay, and it has a long history, and is heading in only one direction: outward and outward to the moment of (self-referential) rupture. Copying creates order, even if what is copied is disorder…." NB stopped mid-sentence. He was looking up at something on the Barn wall: as the camera closed in on it Kaal could see it was a deep curvilinear scratch about 10 centimetres long.

The body on the terrace was moving

inside its black plastic bag. It was less noticeable when the flies were there and nothing on the terrace was still; but during the day, when most were airborne again until the sun went down, there was obvious movement, the plastic seeming to swell and ripple at different points along its length. The shape of it at times suggested that the body might be trying to stand up, that it was in there preparing its limbs, balancing its weight, mustering the required strength from what was left of its muscles. But if the intention was there, nothing so far had come of it, and it remained for the most part flat to the floor. The movement was not dissimilar to that of NB, while asleep under his tarp inside the PsychoBarn, although the comparison was uncomfortable to make.

Most mouths of the living would bubble

with vomit at various points throughout the day. Everyone's vomit the same: a clotted porridge of raw meat and blood, bits of organs. Into cupped hands and straight back inside their mouths was a common tactic, so as not to squander the effort already expended on masticating it, so as not to prolong unnecessarily the unpleasantness of ingestion. For they were eating each other not because they'd developed a taste for themselves overnight, but because there was nothing else, or at least nothing else they could get to, with only a select few, it seemed, having any sort of enthusiasm for the acquisition and consumption of their new diet. From a neo-evolutionary perspective, the human-glutted humans made better, more substantial versions of themselves. Those most proficient at feeding on their own species might one day inherit the earth, and that this earth was already terminal with life made no difference. Who, anyway, was left to purpose the purposeless? Which of them still harboured dreams for the further otherness of themselves when they could barely recognize what they already were? There were some who ate only the vomit, lacking the strength or the will to bite chunks out of the living, and who, if the flies had beaten them to it, ate the maggots they found there as well, with seemingly no more revulsion than had they been absent.

Moreover, he saw people eating glass and bricks and plaster. He saw people pulling birds out the sky on tall buildings and sucking the tiny brains from their skulls one after the other. He saw numerous women, their faces invariably scabrous and sunken, eating their own breasts until there was nothing left.

In this asexualized and digressive parturition, the irrelevance of the sexes in the apparent self-fertilization of both gave rise to the individual's separation from him or herself. From the admixture of the same came the estrangement of the same, difference from sameness and sameness from difference. Each human torn apart from itself, as if to be cured of identity through separation, only to find in that deviant uniqueness a more terrible sickness still: a defilement multiplied and made abstract. From the destruction of the one came the profane and potential immortality of its many.

The woman and her daughter were posi-

tioned outside his door in duplicate. One of the pairs appeared marginally ghosted in comparison to the other. All four of them just stood there staring at the door. He waited for someone to knock but nobody did. He wanted the old man to walk past and imagined the face on him as it registered what had happened. They stood out there for days, and if the old man arrived Kaal wasn't at the fisheye to see it. One day he looked and they'd gone. He had a dream they'd exploded and every tiny particle was a fly. But that hadn't been enough to wake him, so the flies reformed into the mothers and the daughters, only the body parts were in the wrong places. The girls had fingers growing out their mouths and downy pubic hair where their eyes should have been. The skin on their cheeks looked like yellowed toenails. The less faded mother wore a child's vagina in her neck, which she scratched at till it bled. He saw NB stood behind them with stab wounds in his face, mouth wide open like Arbogast, and he woke up. As was usual, he was covered in sweat. The dream was insignificant like all dreams were insignificant, no more no less than the dream of being alive – the dream he was still having, which he'd one day wake from, if the wider universe worked like that and temporal indicators meant anything at all. And he thought of it as a dream, the disarrangement of limbs, digits, hair, etc., the exploding into flies, despite his not having slept for three days, because what else was he going to do with it? You process the world or it processes you, and it already processes you anyway; only, identity is habit-forming and makes demands past the point of credibility, and past the point even of there being anything present to implement such habits. He didn't believe in himself but he was still there, still acting like he did, and if there was a way out he couldn't find it. His looking in the first place seemed to him to enshrine the contradiction of his doubt from the outset. Consequently, he made sense out of what defied it by marking his absence in some way, pushing it somewhere where he wasn't properly present. And then of course he got to thinking: Aren't all lives endured this way?

He was in his fourth week of watching

195 Days... and had become prone in this time to neglecting the terrace and the groundswell below. He returned there to flies up past his ankles, and to more buildings missing and to the storeys of those that remained markedly reduced in number. Somewhat ashamed of what it said about him, he updated his notes. He checked the sky for anything but birds and bugs. He looked over in the direction of the body. He saw the plant there was hidden beneath a caliginous fuzz, alive now with something other than itself. He saw that for all the differences nothing had changed.

The humans still drifted, amassing and dispersing like smog, like cobwebs. They suffocated in the high water of their own bodies. They were their own tides, their own currents. There were no small stories that weren't just the big story, just the monster writhing and farting and shitting all over itself in the service of growth, in the name of being alive.

Although, he was there and had remained separate, away from it in the Tower some distance away, and there must have been others too, others like him who could see the monster without by default seeing themselves – those cursed by their blessings waiting for the thing to come, knowing it's arrived already, the inclusive malediction, waiting for the sake of waiting, for the want of anything else to do so late in the day of what it meant for things to happen.

The frame was sized so as to encompass

the U-shaped area of grass in its entirety. Again the outer reaches of the trees were left outside the extent of its capture, but this time other cameras were trained there just in case – although nothing out of the ordinary will happen. Zooming in on the murder scene revealed no bloodied grass, no residue at all. At the usual hour, out from the west, appeared a woman. Only, once having surfaced from the cover of the trees, she gave no impression of moving any farther. There were no discrepancies between her and the third and fourth woman, for it was easy to ascertain, given her near imperceptible progress across the grass, that in both physical form and dress she and those other women were indistinguishable. She held her left arm across her stomach, securing her nightdress for want of a tie. Everything took its predetermined course according to the pattern of the third and fourth murders, from which the others had deviated in some way; only this time the entire tableau and each of its incremental steps took 12 times longer to complete: 9 minutes for the famous scene, 6.4 minutes for the stabbing to take its course, etc. The stamina, precision and composure of the participants were exemplary. It was hard for him to even imagine how you'd go about choreographing such a thing. Getting the timing right, to the second, in the previous enactments would have been difficult enough, but this... this was inscrutable. The inevitability of what was taking place, while not exactly impaired, was nevertheless transformed into something that extended outside the precincts of a slayed woman, outside all the multitudinous components coming together to realize her repetitively punctured corpse.

The agonizing pace saturated the victim's solo performance in the rectangle with an unalloyed bliss. Every half-second appeared to deliver a fresh ecstasy, a jolting sensation as from a new body, a consciousness revitalized over and over until its fate became unbearable. All those moments lived in such straining abundance, the hands caressing each other, and up and down the length of the opposite arms, the neck craned back to face the sky, mouth open as if a floodgate to let the entire universe in. Her arms stretched in exaltation, and her eyes, as if to reinforce this devotional tone, closed off to the world around her; and yet there was also something inescapably pornographic about the performance, almost as if the cosmos itself was stimulating her from below.

However, for all this pre-murder serenity there remained something fitful and uneasy in the way each movement rubbed up against the next: a jittery idyll, an inharmonious sublime. And it was at this point NB noticed it, as the second figure loomed into view behind her back, to be consolidated with the sweeping horizontal gesture of the murderer's left arm, the ascension of the right, the knife being drawn up and away in preparation for its reversal: something in the inflexible slowness that was altogether too flexible, too open, too spongy in its constitution to prevent him from seeing below its surface, inside it deeper than he should have seen, and once he saw what he saw there was no seeing it the other way, like he'd seen how the illusion worked and could not restore the ignorance he'd lost. And it was the surfeit of time in relation to the relative deprivation of event that allowed it to happen, this sudden porousness, this worm-eaten exterior that required no knife to rupture it. He watched the murky assailant slowly perforate the woman until she was something else, something other than a dying human on the grass. He saw her fold and slide down some imperceptible surface to the ground, and still he wondered, even then, how her stomach muscles, those of her calves and thighs, could have managed such a feat. When finally she collapsed on her front and died, the legs once more decorous for not being apart, there was enough of all the available sadness felt in that single instant to explode his consciousness beyond the possibility of any corrective collapse. And yet, the dead body lay there like a grace upon the line made of light that it traversed. The slow retreat of the murderer an unfortunate embellishment, so crude in its purpose he could barely look. He lingered on the last few seconds of her dead body like the green lights would eradicate more than just the scene in front of him.

The following night he would watch the same events transpire at the same excruciating pace. He would confirm what he had seen. He would be unable to return from where he ended up.

From the terrace, the colours and the

patterns of the people looked iridescent, prismatic, like oil displaced on water; or else a hydra with however many quadrillion heads, some rotted out some living, most unseen, all disproportionately human.

The AC was failing, working only in short blasts and then emitting only feeble exhalations insufficiently cooled. But even in the 90-degree-plus heat, with the air around the vents no better than tepid, Kaal's skin was raised on every follicle, his body wracked by a series of micro-convulsions indicative of some other lesser temperature. He sat in his chair waiting for the green flashes to clear.

NB was silent. Had they witnessed the same thing? Kaal could hear his strained breathing above the noise of the city: its traffic, the birds spiralling upwards in a tumult, the teenagers screaming in the park. As it became increasingly laboured he imagined him engaged in some act of extreme and agonizing exertion, everything from weighted chin-ups to chopping off a limb. There was an increasing need to see what NB was doing, what state he was in. And with his agitation approaching panic, a face came into frame, a face he didn't immediately recognize as being that of NB, a face that ran through him like an electrical charge, at which point there was no longer any doubt that what Kaal had seen had been more than some hallucinatory quirk of light, more than the imaginings of a man sequestered in a tower waiting for a giant human monster the size of Mumbai to eat him alive; for whatever he'd seen, this face had seen it too, this face that while sharing the approximate arrangement of NB's was now mutated into some piteous and corrupted likeness, identity having degraded so rapidly as to find itself transformed into the shakiest of resemblances. And yet it was him. There was still enough left for Kaal to be fairly certain of a noxious continuity between the man on the screen and the man there some few minutes before. In fact, his looking so unlike himself, retaining only those structural relations vital to this comparative recognition, made it somehow more feasible that it was actually him, the distortion to his features correlating perfectly in some unmeasurable sense with what had happened moments earlier.

As he looked at NB's ravaged countenance he wondered if his own face had undergone similar modifications, or whether as his touching seemed to confirm, nothing significant had changed.

Most of the original fluid in the barrels

had been displaced, with any that remained filling only the most negligible of spaces left between and inside the more recent items of ballast that had gradually supplanted it. Like vinegar in a pickling jar now, only it didn't preserve but instead turned increasingly murky and toxic, the objects enveloped there leaching into it, the water darkening, thickening, becoming rancid. Even with the lids of the barrels replaced the smell of the contents escaped, drifting through and around the house where it marbled the air with its unpleasant sweetness.

The barrels and the accumulating ballast sequestered elsewhere about the house started to attract flies. More and more the visitors were under the impression that Parker was replicating the imagined stench of the exhumed mother, or of Ed Gein's exotic tastes in home furnishings. Some thought it was the smell of the conveniently located swamp, here supposedly positioned somewhere outside the perimeter of the Met roof, wafting in on an artificially made breeze for the purposes of contextualization and the dissuasion of impromptu lunch parties. An increase in the number of birds was also notable, enticed no doubt by the flies and the scraps of food carelessly discarded by NB over recent weeks. They occupied the edges of the roof and those interior poles situated above head-height.

In the mornings the terrace was sticky

underfoot with fly shit. Every night he placed the nozzle-end of the hose by the sliding doors so he could spray an area clean before stepping outside. Although it was usually mid-morning already by the time he came to wash the terrace down, the daily exodus of flies was never so comprehensive as to leave only the black speckling of their faeces behind, and a remainder of the lethargic and the dead would also be invariably sluiced away with it.

The use of flies in waste management was something given serious consideration and even implemented at one time. Fly larvae (species specific according to waste) would effectively recycle the nutrient content of mankind's surplus by breaking down the offending material before then either becoming a nourishing animal feed or of use in the production of secondary products such as biodiesel, any residual waste being transformed into an effective fertilizer. Maggots utilized this way could reduce the offensive deoxygenated slimes of decay, and the inevitable stench of methane, producing instead a dry and alkaline environment that was virtually odour free. But the flies for all their number could no longer effect such change.

There were many more birds now and the way they perched – so still, so unobtrusive, the faint humming sound they made – it was easy to mistake them for cameras. Most were predictably itinerant and very much interchangeable, but others once there were reluctant to move, regardless of how much NB swung his arms in their vicinity. They became permanent fixtures, barely stirring, the eyes open watching no matter what time of day or night. Knowing what they represented, he came to ignore them. They explained themselves silently as pertinent background features to be considered in conjunction with other salient details without distracting from a core diegetic trajectory, in comparison to which they were mere dust. Sometimes they allowed themselves to become covered in flies, and he noticed them again as if for the first time. He became less certain then about the relative importance of any of the numerous events happening in and around the house at any one time. It was at these precarious intervals that he retreated to a particular spot in the structure's left facade, pressed his face up against the reddened wood and left it there for a duration made indeterminate by the use of cuts in post-production.

The GMS building looks like a spaceship

has landed in the heart of Mumbai was a line, either in exact or paraphrastic form, he'd read and heard repeated often around the time of its construction. Like a spaceship has landed in Mumbai. Like a spaceship has landed between the Dharavi slum and the business district, because if it wasn't from a place other than earth what would it be doing there, with its appearance seemingly borrowed from both, as if desperate to fit in, and yet strikingly incongruous to the architecture of the city – to the architecture of the planet, even? And presuming the Japanese girl in São Paulo was not the first splitter, but only the first to be recorded and shared worldwide, there was a case to be made, albeit supported only anecdotally, for 15-year-old dabbawalla, Ram Sumer, in his parent's single-room dwelling off Rajendra Prasad Chawl being the first, dividing some three and a half weeks before the Brazil video went viral, and who's to say the two arrivals weren't connected.

From the lane to the railroad shanties, from the recycling area to the pipes, the slum was alive with news of the boy who'd developed an extra set of arms before becoming two of himself, who'd summoned Shiva, then Vishnu, then Brahma then Hanuman. The boy-deity of Dharavi, whose second manifestation was divested of all genital traces, the slum child expediting his ascension to moksha via autoproliferation, via his increased samsaric burden. The boy gave hope beyond the gains of any one day, beyond the machinations of staying alive, the frayed fiduciary strings of commerce, the generational inertia, beyond even the slum's sanitary deficiencies and the threat of fire, flood and disease, risked as a way of life minute by minute. Ram Sumer: godboy, saviour of ghosts, maker and reconciler of pain. Ram Sumer (such an unhappy name, the father of that murdered boy): the world's first splitter, though largely uncredited outside Mumbai, outside Dharavi, gave himself another mouth to put food inside, and no distance away the GMS building looking like a spaceship had landed, aliens in the cantilevers, drugging souls behind the shaded fenestrae, in there remotely reconfiguring human biology according to whim, or else in line with some unknown and possibly unknowable agenda – perhaps both.

The flies around the tops of the barrels

started drawing attention. NB heard them mentioned with increasing frequency, with some even wondering if they were real, and others postulating on what could be inside the barrels to attract them in such numbers. After a few days of listening it seemed the consensus was that they were "an interesting flourish," a "nice touch," an "artistic conceit" to remind the audience of the grubby reality of the PsychoBarn's mythos.

And so he prepared to be discovered, even contemplated leaving before they arrived; however, despite the growing sense that his discovery was already overdue, he remained, lacking any motivation to leave or sense of where he might go if he did. There was only what he was doing and the agonizing mystery of that alone – which had in turn been transformed into the mystery of everything else. He could stay where he was and accept what remained of the 195 days as also his own duration, or… or else posit the existence of an outside that notwithstanding from the imminent threat seemed too distant now to imagine let alone inhabit.

He waited for the maintenance crew to arrive, for Parker herself, even, for someone to come and inspect the barrels and find therein the reason for this much-discussed infestation. But while the flies kept coming, swarming at times around the roof like tiny starlings, and the visitors too kept admiring their authenticity, their invocation of the swamp, their "sculptural and conceptual fluidity," nobody else came.

NB had stopped eating, or else was ingesting

just enough to stay alive. His food supplies were piling up in the interior front corner of the Barn, the insides of the transparent ziplock bags beading with condensation in the sun. When the screen began dividing into a grid to show the footage from every camera at once, all angles covered as if part of some large-scale surveillance operation, Kaal was forced to change the playback settings on his media player in an effort to keep up. He watched NB move from one box to the next, dragging himself aimlessly through the triangulated grid system of the scaffold poles, one reticulation inside another, and him there prowling in a spiral motion, expanding and contracting as the limits of the PsychoBarn dictated. Where the lids of the barrels were no longer sealed tight – thin openings apparent now on each one – streaky water dribbled over the edges and down the sides, with flies collecting in increasing numbers in and around the gaps and on the floor around their bases.

Sinewy men in shorts and sandals, necks

flexing inside heavy chains, their arms upraised to support their giant heads – heads 100 times the size at least of the standard human kind, and each one held together with string and ragged cloth – hustled down crudely-fashioned streets to where they got to take them off, at which point new heads had to be found, each one's parts assembled along the way, to be brought back to the same place and once again abandoned with the many other heads just like it.

Kaal remembered the second slum division, itself preceding the Brazil case by more than a week, remembered going there in some made up capacity ("I'm from the university, come to document…") to see for himself whether the end he'd imagined was being imagined elsewhere in the minds of others, or was being imagined instead by the bodies themselves. He remembered getting lost in there, amongst homes like Dali faces propped up on sticks, their walls and roofs made of corrugated metal, the rusting, the perished plaster, the rotting bricks, barrels out to catch the rain, the rustle of doors and windows made from blue tarpaulin, the clothes and babies drying in the streets, the giant heads in rows and the old men in white shirts that guarded them on old wooden chairs. He remembered how the men's clothing was invariably dull, while the women's was mostly brightly coloured, how it was the opposite of birds. The Muslim women, dressed in black, were the exception, with just their eyes on show, gliding through the filthy, litter-bestrewn alleyways like the solar occlusions of Indian princesses. In his ears the sound of electric fans and voices and car horns and machinery, of a dog chewing on the hind leg of an unattended goat. He remembered how the impressions the people there did of contentment were more convincing than anywhere else he'd been, almost as if the mimesis had turned into the thing it was copying – almost.

It was ten or so children that eventually showed him the way to the Rani residence, the part-pallet wood part-brick one-room home of the split mother and her three daughters, Dalits who had nevertheless felt the touch of God, seen him, as if from a distance much larger than the room, pull a second mother out the already wasted body of the first. They talked excitedly all the way there, asking for things he didn't have, offering things he didn't want, laughing over and over at his having been lost, a university professor, as if thinking men losing their way was the most absurd circumstance they could imagine. He tried to explain how though he'd been born in India he'd left when he was young and hadn't been back all that long; but they weren't interested in his excuses, pretending not to hear, lest they should impede the momentum of their goading.

Some of the children had bite marks on their arms and legs, from the rats they said, that ate them in their sleep. Some had toes and fingers missing. One claimed his mother still had the bones from the digits that were gone, and that sometimes she would look at them to make herself cry.

The boys, who had run ahead and into the woman's home to apprise her of his coming, were being shooed out as he arrived. One of the daughters, dressed in a calf-length gown of an implausibly iridescent cerise, waited in the doorway, her head down waving him inside. To the closest boy he handed ⊠20, and watched as he ran off with it into a narrow-gutted passageway, the others on him in an instant, all of them gone before he'd turned and ducked to enter the room.

The mother and two of her daughters were sat on a metal-framed bed running along the wall to his left, soon to be joined by the third daughter, who sat on the end closest to the door. What remained of the bed's blue paint, most of it having peeled back to the dull grey of the metal underneath, matched that of the wall behind them, which though primarily the same pale blue looked darker and bubbled in places, as if the room's one brick wall wasn't brick at all but layers of paper that someone had been setting fire to. The remaining three walls were botched together with strips of packing wood, many of which had warped and split to reveal the colour of the tarp outside, also of a similar blue.

They all four pointed to a chair to his right, and barely having straightened again since entering he sat down. In the opposite corner to the entrance was a second chair where another woman was sat, a woman he took to be the second mother. When he looked at her the rest of them made a point of looking the other way, in the direction of the door, as if to say: you look, we understand, but we have seen enough. She sat hunched and coiled in a length of drab fabric looking at the floor. Her glances upward were furtive and always to the mother, the sentiments expressed therein a mixture, it seemed to him, of mildly deranged curiosity and dread.

The youngest daughter stared at the TV on the wall at the end of the bed. It was switched off, but from the way she looked at it you couldn't tell. The rest of the Rani family, now that he had turned his attention away from the woman in the corner, were looking somewhere in the vicinity of his head, but not directly at him, waiting for their guest to speak. He felt the onus on him to explain his presence there, to introduce himself at least, but the additional mother, crumpled in the corner like an abused animal had put him off his game, and the more he thought about speaking the less forthcoming were the words required to do it.

How he eventually spoke was a surprise to him, so much so it felt like he'd been ventriloquized, only becoming properly conscious of his preamble as it was nearing its end. He was unnerved in that moment to the point of running out the room, but the woman in the corner somehow kept him there: the way she was looking, right at him, the face so broken down, the eyes asking something of him, or else trying to convey something – he couldn't tell which.

He looked up and saw that the corrugated metal roof was resting on seven scaffold poles so arranged as to form two squares, each divided obliquely through the middle into two isosceles triangles. He was still looking at the ceiling as the mother on the bed started to explain how generous people had been since the event, bringing food, new clothes, bits of furniture, and the TV on the wall that so completely gorgonized the youngest daughter. Others though, she said, had stopped visiting since it happened, old friends, one in particular: an elderly man who used to take care of the girls. Not the father, no, but what sounded like a benefactor of sorts: nice man, kind man. She searched behind her on the bed for a picture she had, maybe he knew him. He couldn't see why he would, and overriding her frantic rummaging turned the conversation back to the details of the event itself.

Without turning round, or only intermittently, she said how it was the best thing, a gift, that the family had been blessed that day, the best thing, the best thing. He noticed how the woman in the corner, now looking at the floor, was shaking her head about all over the place as if to dislodge something from her ears, or given the vigour of the movements perhaps the head itself. He asked if they all thought it was the best thing, to which the girls nodded in unison, the two eldest reaching for their mother's hands, to be received greedily and squeezed with such filial tenderness that he was reluctant to pursue any further the doubts that he was having. And yet he broached the question again, this time to the woman in the corner, addressing her as Mrs Rani. He saw some contortion round the mouth of the Mrs Rani on the bed, saw her go to speak and then stop, frustrated, angered, he thought. The woman in the corner was looking at the floor now and did not look up, her head still oscillating with an uncommon violence.

"She won't talk," said the daughter closest to the door, "she never talks, not anymore."

"She used to talk before it happened?" he asked, and she went to nod and stopped halfway, turning in a burgeoning panic in the direction of the mother sat next to her and to whose hand she was still attached.

"Best thing for all of us," the mother interjected, pulling her daughters closer.

The woman in the corner had stopped moving her head. She was looking at him as intently as he was looking anywhere else but back at her. How could he return her gaze now? How could his eyes console? How could they reveal anything but the discursive evasions of his thoughts, as they studied all the elements of the small room in quick and repetitive succession: shelved items (pristine pots and pans, screwtop jars and plates, base metal moulds of Hindu icons), blotches in the paintwork, small tapestries, a calendar, carrier bags hanging off nails, intermittently lit striplights, fabrics pendant from the ceiling.

A deep groaning noise came from her direction. The rest of the family talked over the sound like it wasn't happening, like they were nervous it might come to form words and sentences, and that from them they might be incriminated further. They talked at once and tangentially, making it difficult for him to reply, or even at times to keep up with what was being said. His neck seeming less rigid at this point, more like a fluid, as he essayed a smile, his disequilibrium matching he thought that of the woman, whose head was once again gesticulating chaotically between her rounded shoulders.

"It arrived inside that building: the GMS. When it landed. It's been waiting and now this. It's just the beginning. It's just the beginning."

The mother on the bed laughed. The daughter to her right, suspecting him a credulous type, said that buildings do not land but are built, and how it's nothing but office workers in there. The other two daughters looked ill at ease, as if they too thought the GMS might be to blame for the predicament of having an extra mother.

When, some half-hour or so later, he got up to leave, the mother from the bed handed him a photograph. He hadn't seen the man before and said so and went to give it back. She told him to keep it, pushing his hand away. Maybe he'd see him, tell him to come again. The likelihood being so absurdly slight he continued to gesture that she take it back. But she had others, she said, and he should take it just in case. He might see him, tell him to come. He gave up, folded the photograph in half and put it in his trouser pocket.

Back outside the boys were waiting for him. They escorted him in the direction of the harbour-line bridge. He showed the photograph to a boy of about ten immediately to his right. He took it, looked at it closely for a few seconds and just shrugged. As he was handing it back, another, older boy snatched it from his hand. He knew him, he said, got confirmation from two more boys, all of whom agreed: a dirty fucker, weird spazzed out bastard, queer shit, nasty reptile cunt.

It was like watching himself dying, on
the Met roof, years earlier. He became increasingly devitalized. It was harder now for him to take regular breaks from the

screen. When NB talked it sounded like his own thoughts rigged up to his laptop speaker. Who he was was becoming diluted in that room. He used to dream of being this numb, this analytically recursive. The loop tightened but the space inside it stayed the same.

There was a faint knocking sound coming

from inside one of the barrels, perhaps more than one. NB had spent all morning going from one barrel to the next, his ear pressed against their sides, listening. His face was still the same partially imploded version of itself it had been since the seventh and eighth murders in the park; only now all traces of shock had been transposed by a dull, haunted consistency, a lived-in consolidation of that day's anathema, and those endured since. As for his own face, Kaal was yet to look, not wanting to see, feeling with his hands a worsening subsidence to the muscle tone there, but risking no further confirmation as to its degraded state.

The terrace overhang drooled its black

stalactiform deposits onto the decking, hundreds of thousands of flies like threadbare drapes sliding down the outsides of the sliding doors.

Kaal stood over the body and watered the plants. Some water splashed off the dry soil and onto the body's covering of black plastic. Placing the still half-full water can beside the body's head, he returned to the edge of the terrace and watched a fair-skinned boy, aged about ten, becoming himself again in another place just outside his original body. The boy quailed and stammered and wet his shorts, a pale blue turning almost black. He watched a bank of dark clouds drift across the skyline from the terrace off bedroom 3.

The camera passed over about a week's worth of his bagged waste. This neglect of procedure was less surprising than it otherwise would have been, given the turn his soliloquies had been taking for at least that long. He ate now in a trance, bringing the food up to his mouth without bothering to look at it, combining flavours randomly as if there was no one left to taste them. When he talked, the intonation was missing, each word part of the same droning uniformity, lacking telos and origin in equal measure. He talked of occupying the present as if it were a mode of incarceration, a windowless interior filled with nothing but the sound of his own breathing.

Of the skyscrapers clearly visible from the Tower (Raheja Imperia/Atlantis, World Crest, Palais Royale...), all but the tallest had succumbed. Not having been sealed off in time to protect their top floors, they swiftly became infested with thousands of humans all collected into a single mass and oozing through doors, rooms and windows like a semi-conscious slime.

Over in Worli, transcending the skyline by some few hundred feet, was the Mumbai Television Tower, its red and white open latticework structure coated right up to its acicular apex with those left healthy and agile enough to climb that high. Through his binoculars he saw them filling the tubular structure running up its core and clinging to and ascending its slanted uprights; eventually, the crude encampments made on the various-sized layers inside its many inverted pyramids, and on the square-based platforms shrinking in size the higher it rose from the ground, obscured all but the tower's external structure. Others like the Namaste Tower were sinking more slowly, their smooth facades proving resistant to exterior scaling.

Only three of the many skyscrapers in clear view showed obvious signs of having isolated their upper floors from the rising glut of bodies below. At the top, he could see lights and signs of life. Although, even through his binoculars he could not zoom close enough to see details, only vague silhouettes of people calm in their movements, navigating the space of their apartments in ways that, while standardized, now felt anything but. He saw what looked like the light from TV screens. He wondered whether they had noticed him, and figured they probably had, though he never saw any hint of them looking in his direction. He thought about the possibilities of making contact, putting together a sign large enough for them to read and to which they would then feel compelled to reply. But when it came down to what he might write that was worth conveying nothing presented itself. What could he say? What could they reply? He worked through innumerable permutations of these imagined exchanges and not one of them was worth the effort of enacting. No practical answer to their common bind could be reached. They passed their imagined observations to and fro and none of it amounted to anything: no one was in a position to assist themselves or anyone else. All it could be was company for the death (or worse) that was coming, and who needed that?

The proximity of other humans was not what he needed; what he needed was the exact opposite of that. And entailed in that distance was a solution to whatever this was that had happened and to his existing as he did in the midst of it. In other words, he wanted a solution to himself. In other words, regardless of what had happened to the world around him, nothing substantial had changed, and this itself was a predicament, an old one, reframed but essentially the same. The point of being alive *then* was the point of being alive *now*: the same eternal ellipsis occluded by the incessant demands and functionality of a body (however many versions of it there were) that stays alive for the sake of it, as if existence were an art (disguised as drudgery).

The horror remained inside, compounded by his own facility for division but interior in the earlier sense too: horror at the biology, the dirty work that he didn't see and that had no regard for that non-thing supervening on its continued industry. And while it was a horror to which he was anaesthetized, there was still that inflexible feeling of disgust and a wearying disconnect. For although his circumstances were extraordinary, he remained indentured to the same crushing normality that, for all its influence, could never quite ingratiate itself to the point where it dispelled the core alterity of his existing as anything at all, anywhere, ever.

NB became increasingly fixated on Marion's wounds. He sketched diagrammatic outlines of her body, like you'd find in a medical examiner's report, on which he marked the stab wounds from all the different versions of her murder, some of which he had to guess. Because he could never be sure of the exact number or placement for any one of the three variations, he repeated the exercise over and over in an attempt to account for all the most likely renderings. He would lay them out around him and compare and contrast the myriad arrangements, identifying where possible correlations and patterns suggestive of deeper significance. He saw no end to it. The import of the dead 8, the forever recumbent 8, would only grow, could only fulfill its promised infinitude. There was no retreat to a conclusion; there was only the continued spread of trauma and of bodies – and ultimately the trauma of embodiment itself.

Sat cross-legged in the main internal corner of the Barn, NB spoke to many cameras at once, his eyes shifting, scarcely more than glancing in the direction of any one of them, his attention focused almost exclusively on the areas between. It was late evening and his face was artificially lit by a nearby torch. The crotch of his trousers was soaking wet and there was a quantity of what looked to be urine pooling around his feet. He talked at a volume that evidenced his newfound resolve concerning the inconsequence of his being overheard. He talked as if every minute of his existence was concentrated in this one brief outburst: "We are all of us the blood from Marion's wounds. When we witness Her naked vulnerability in the shower we are watching nature failing to bring us about, to realize who we are. Her resistance to being punctured is our own unpreparedness for being born, and it is only through Her lacerations that we are released. We escape Her constraining network, the centrality of Her conflicted heart, and once free forget all burden of origins. Her blood is alien blood. We change: we become. We are as connected in our differences as we are in our similarities. The flood will not wash us away, for we are the flood."

There were days when the flies amassed in choking swathes. They would crawl up underneath his plastic sheet and he'd find them in his ears and in his mouth when he woke up. He would hear visitors coughing them up and complaining to each other and to museum staff about how their lunches were being spoiled, and lost count of how many were found drowning in wine glasses. The bags of his waste piled in the corner grew a carpet of the things, and still nobody came to see what was causing it – almost as if they knew and were expecting them, almost as if the flies (and perhaps…) were part of the installation.

For some reason unattended by reasons of its own he'd felt prematurely compelled to watch what remained of *195 Days…* to its end in one go. He thought, looking back, that he'd sensed from the beginning that the film contained parallels with and implications for what was coming that were too uncanny to ignore; but part of him couldn't help seeing this as mere retrospective gloss, and that the more likely reason was their shared segregation, both being conspicuously aberrant and banal in equal measure.

While he had no interest in communicating with the people he'd seen in the other towers, there was still the compulsion to watch them, to see what preparations they were making, if any, but most importantly to get a clear view of what happened when the ground rose up and engulfed them. And yet he already knew without watching, having seen so many other structures yield over recent days and weeks, how it went, how it would go, how like rocks when the tide came in they would just disappear, and how this tide, incapable of retreat, swallowed buildings with no thought of ever regurgitating them again.

He wanted to watch because the others had been no more than structures, just bricks and glass and steel ceasing to be visible; whereas these people were surviving like he was surviving, in quarantine, in normalcy, and so their demise was also his. In other words, he wanted to watch his own death before it happened. But even this was an idealistic formulation, for death most likely would not be instantaneous, but an eked out ordeal of slow suffocation, partial dismemberment, starvation and disease. The unimaginable nothingness of his own nonexistence would have to wait – and feeling, as it always had, both inevitable and impossible, he'd been preparing all this time to wait forever.

Flies dripped from the terrace overhang.

The body, still shrouded in its black plastic bag, was upright in the middle of the main terrace, walking in small circles, less than a metre in diameter, stopping and starting at irregular intervals. The body was enveloped in the bag all the way down to the knees, below which its legs could be seen, the bottoms of its dark grey trousers, the shoes missing, its bare feet yellowed and blackened at the soles. The body stood just under 6 foot, shortened a few inches by a defined stoop. He watched the shuffling figure from behind the sliding glass doors. He made a sloshing, gurgling sound with his mouth as the body went about its restricted circuits, stopping when the body stopped. The body's feet cleared a rough circle in the flies. Others could be seen crawling up his legs and underneath the cover of the black plastic bag.

There was something he was missing, something NB had come to know, something hinted at, divulged only in part by the seventh and eighth murders, that if he too could become cognizant of it the questions would disappear, the latter instalments of the film becoming clear as a consequence. But he wondered, and this shredded his nerves more than any thought of the horde, whether the price of this clarity would be the same as that paid by NB, a price he couldn't possibly quantify until it was already paid.

Although *Psycho* was clearly Manichaean, with its many doublings and specular gestures having been well documented by various observant cineastes over the years, it wasn't any of the standard examples that troubled NB: not that Marion is mirrored in turn by Sam and Norman, or that Marion's bras and purses (going from white to black) signal a fundamental revision of her character, or that Marion's confliction is revealed in the mirrors in her apartment, in the car lot restroom, and motel room 1, or that Norman is both himself and his mother, or that that seamless rotating optical is of Marion's eye, or even that the filming of the shower scene involves two murdered bodies (a stabbed Janet Leigh and a dead showgirl, Marli Renfro, for the curtain grab and the clean-up). Nor did he consider it important that the dead were seen to come back to life, as Mother does in Norman, as would happen in a zombie plague. And while he described it at some length, it was also only of passing interest that while entertaining Marion in his parlour and discussing his love of taxidermy, Norman's right arm is raised up like a wing (the arm that will stab her to death in just over 10 minutes), as if to say "I am only half of this stuffed bird." No, NB saw something else happening: he saw instead the creeping irrelevance of these divisions, and of all and every attempt at separation.

When you take living things apart to see

how they work, and you are sufficiently diligent and comprehensive in that dismemberment, you do not find a neat and cogent arrangement of interconnecting parts: you find instead a putrid ooze – you find the insides of a cockroach.

All eight times NB had witnessed something approximating what *Psycho* screenwriter Joseph Stefano had referred to as the "heartbreaking shot." The original shot was cut from the 1960 film to appease the censors: the shot being an overhead of Marion's naked body slumped over the edge of the bath with her rear exposed – a shot reinstated by Van Sant. According to Stefano, this "one shot really brought home the tragedy of lost life," claiming he had "never seen anything more painful than to see that beauty murdered. It was so poetic and so hurtful." Kaal too could feel the heartbreak now, could feel it like it was the only emotion he had left. Only, even the wrench of that was tempered with intrigue, for on that eighth occasion there'd been something else to contend with, for he was certain he'd seen emerging out of the body's back end some indistinct entity that appeared to slowly crawl down the inside of her left leg.

For all its metaphysical and aesthetic ambiguities, the video work posed more pragmatic questions. These were concerned, for the most part, with its veracity, its credibility as a reliable document of what had happened on and around the Met roof over those 195 days. The most obstinate niggle for Kaal was why, when the Barn was dismantled, had the sensational details of what was found there not been widely publicized. Or if indeed it had been made public, how had he not heard about it. Surrounding these core anxieties were a litany of only marginally less substantial improbabilities: How, given his behaviour, had he not been discovered? Why were there no other reported sightings of the nightly murders in Central Park? Where was the list of missing artists and writers last seen or heard from some time before visiting the PscyhoBarn? Why had the film's post-production taken so long to complete? And what explained the low-key manner and timing of that eventual release? Watching NB on screen, it seemed facile to doubt that his engagement was anything but genuine. Even with all these inconsistencies in the forefront of his mind, it still seemed to him interminably more absurd to think of NB's reactions as being some kind of performance. That the whole thing had been green-screened in some warehouse and that NB had simply acted out a role, as of an artist unpicking the nature of horror as duplication, which in turn had disassembled him, was in many ways the most comprehensive and obvious answer. And yet that wasn't what he'd seen. He was certain of it. For while feeling uneasy about the certainty itself, which he couldn't properly explain, there was no want for conviction when it came to the reality of that certainty. But then if it was real, all the questions remained, questions that the vigour of his persuasion, formidable as it was, did not equip him to answer.

There was a clue and he was missing it.

It would be there in the film, in the shower scene, in the many re-enactments. That the shower scene was regarded by some film theorists as an assault on female sexuality, as too was this apocalypse of non-maternal division, was not enough – was insufficiently direct. That Norman might be thought of as two people in one, or as a son who gives birth to his own mother, or that Marion is repeatedly doubled in mirrors, or that Lila is seen in triplicate in Norma's bedroom, that the murdered Marion and the dead Marion are two different women, that Norma's voice is three people's voices and her body at least five, that the opposing diagonal lines of the knife and the water spray from the shower are indicative of division, that the shower and the knife were presaged by the rain and the wiper-blades, that vertical compositions are used to suggest confinement, etc. was none of it immediate enough to amount to an unequivocal clue. That our perspective is first with Marion (one person whose only double is a reflection), before switching to Norman (two persons occupying the same body), and finally to that of Lila and Sam (two distinct persons), was suggestive but added up, he thought, to little more than a taunt. It was all broadly redolent of where he was at without pinpointing any explicit connection. While it was tempting to expand on these correlations, he resisted in favour of searching out the one link that would extirpate all doubt.

He'd been watching *195 Days…* now for

the majority of his exile, and while his days had been filled more variously than had he been exclusive in his viewing, the diurnal commitment had been observed without aberration. But it happened when it happened as if from nowhere. He was watching the first victim dispose of those all too familiar scraps of paper into the representation of a toilet for the nth time when, without warning, he stopped breathing. He sat there waiting for his airways to open, the thought he'd had germinating till it filled his head: "It's ridiculous!" he averred to himself. The writing down of such a simple calculation was absurd. 40,000 minus 700: a child could do it in their head.

There must, he thought, be some other reason for its inclusion. Most obvious was its function as a narrative device: a scrap of the torn-up calculation being subsequently discovered by Lila, from which she and Sam are able to confirm that Marion did indeed stop at the Bates Motel. But this was far too clumsy for the Master of Suspense, the purveyor of pure cinema; and just maybe the money wasn't the MacGuffin everyone took it to be. She could just have easily left behind a small item of jewellery, a distinctive button, say; or have written something else, something more credible, the plan of her excuse perhaps. But instead, she wrote down a calculation that nobody, even those with the most rudimentary mathematical ability, would need to write down. Its inelegance as a diegetic stratagem was both unquestionable and unlikely. Kaal was convinced, therefore, that it must serve another purpose, must symbolize something else entirely. He wrote out the sum as seen on a scrap of paper, minus the + digits obscured by her hand:

40,000
  700
39,300

The numbers in Van Sant's sequel were different, to account for the time value of money and the fact that Marion was hardly likely to risk her job and her liberty for a measly $40,000. With this in mind, Stefano and Van Sant upped the amount to $400,000. But there was another detail in the revised calculation that was significantly more interesting, a detail that indicated that Van Sant knew that by changing the calculation he was also removing its primary justification. The numbers in Van Sant's version were as follows:

400,000
  4,036
395,963

Although this time we see the + digits, no further calculation is made, and so, as with the original, it's as if the point has been made without having to go any further. Both 39,300 and 395,963 would not have to symbolize anything else if the + digits below went on to form a continuation of the sum, but they don't. It could be argued that, exasperated about how far short she is of making good the deficit, she simply abandons her calculations in defeat. However, if we're to believe that she is so atrocious with figures that she needs to do the original calculation (40,000 minus 700), then why should we be convinced that she can calculate the remaining deficit in her head almost instantaneously? Also, we must remember that only the number of the stolen amount – 40,000 and 400,000 respectively – will resonate with Lila and Sam when they come to find it. This is why, as a plot device, the original figure needs to be written, as opposed to her just doing the calculation in her head and starting with 39,300 or 395,963. And admittedly, Van Sant's version of the sum is not quite as ridiculously straightforward as the original. But even so, Van Sant feels the need to reference its credibility by having her make a subtracting error: 400,000 minus 4,036 is not 395,963 but 395,964. And yet, despite referencing her poor head for figures, she too is able to do the final calculation in her head, confidently, in about a second. There's confusion here and it stems from the fact that in the original film the sum's use as a plot device is only secondary, and something else is being conveyed in those numbers: a clue, a message, a confirmation.

Kaal spun the piece of paper around with his index finger on the coffee table, emulating the roiling of flushed toilet water. He stopped and stared out at the body on the terrace. He watched it walking in circles covered in flies. He looked back at the paper, at the figures upside down, and there it was: OOEbE.

'OO' he recognized as a prefix denoting egg or ovum, the germ or seed of something, but EBE? What was EBE?

He recognized that too, but couldn't think where from. An acronym? Yes, an acronym for sure, but for what? From something read recently, something since the acceleration, perhaps one of the sites expounding innumerable theories as to why humans had suddenly turned amoebic. He picked his laptop off the sofa beside him and started to root through numerous files filled with text culled from sites before they went down. It took 20 minutes or so, but there it was: EBE (Extra-terrestrial Biological Entity).

He felt the muscles in his face tighten. He watched his legs moving up and down in relay, the laptop rested there rocking from side to side. His body knew the significance of this finding and it trembled and tensed around it.

He told himself that this was not just some case of apophenia contracted out of desperation. He told himself that this explained the otherwise suspiciously awkward plot device. And yet, if *Psycho* was the self-proclaimed egg (or seed) of this apocalypse by division, how did it happen? How could that even be possible? Could he actually believe the film played a causal role? And if so, what? As usual, the answer just proved to be the germ of yet more questions.

But that it was hidden and that it was flushed away, as if Hitchcock himself could not bear to look at it, to acknowledge its existence even, should come as no surprise from someone so pathologically disgusted by the material composition of an egg: "I'm frightened of eggs, worse than frightened; they revolt me. That white round thing without any holes and when you break it, inside there's that yellow thing, round, without any holes… Brrr!"

The first part of *Psycho*, up until Marion's murder, has been called a red herring, as has the Bates dwelling itself, which, constructed to resemble some haunted house, leads the viewer to expect the presence of some supernatural evil, rather than the very human evil embodied by Norman. But Kaal wondered now whether the house was less of a red herring than it seemed, and whether this allusion to the otherworldly was instead an indication of the film's deeper intelligence. If, as Hitchcock believed, the effect of realism relies on unreality, then maybe his current reality was equally reliant on the unreal. Could it be that the masking on the interneg, to obscure Marion's breasts, was only one tiny fraction of the things *Psycho* was masking? But then, yes... the film itself, it was the film itself, and all its many reincarnations... the red herring was not any one part of the film, but the film in its entirety. *Psycho* itself was the subterfuge. But what was being hidden?

The maggot mass on a nearby rooftop looked to be several feet deep. It struggled against itself like a body of water with a thousand different currents. That and a thickening slick of adipocere made staying upright difficult for the fit and close to impossible for the rest. Spiders the size of hands darted like monsters over the backs of ants and flies. A lizard sat on a dead woman's face eating a yellow butterfly. There were different breeds of snakes navigating the human gunk in search of bloated rats, their bellies full of rotting people, their senses dulled by it. The trees were bristling with shrikes filling up on flies. He imagined he could hear the sound of maggots at work, their digestive enzymes breaking down healthy tissues, the sounds of fats decomposing, of men and women vanishing beneath their own insane multitudes.

There were mounds of pupating maggots in the bottoms of human ribcages. They resembled abandoned offerings of flavoured rice. They were eaten by birds, by people. Layers of skeletonized corpses were being flattened under the weight of the partially decomposed, the freshly dead, the dying. And above this crust of the gone were those still alive and doubling, building with their own flesh a sprawling Tower of Babel, wherein the single language was a scream. Somewhere inside was the remembered scream of those first audiences of *Psycho*, the shriek of Marion about to be murdered, Lila in the fruit cellar, Herrmann's score.

The smell from the bodies was thick in the air, the flies more each day. All the additional cameras could not be hidden at a moment's notice, and the bags and the bottles filled with his waste amassed in the corner with no regard for who might see them. And yet he was not discovered. He continued there unnoticed. Kaal couldn't work it out. And the 8 murders in Central Park. Too fantastic, all of it. He was increasingly inclined to believe that the shower reenactments had been a publicity stunt, a complimentary fringe event in response to the PsychoBarn – organized perhaps by MC herself. No other explanation seemed credible.

Kaal sat there listening to NB's head

coming apart, sat there watching as his face, increasingly precarious, strained to accommodate the heteroglossia of some unseen multitude. NB's head looked to be both on the brink of shattering and built from the hastily reformed fragments of a head that had already shattered. Like it hovered between those two states. Like it was both exploding and imploding at the same time. The sound he made seemed less derived from language than from the low-frequency screeching of deepwater fish.

Kaal noticed how the indent in Norma's

bed – of a corpse on its side, knees raised up, arm stretched out in front – was also the shape of one half of a human body, divided down the middle. He remembered how Ed Gein had 5 spare faces, ones removed from other people, sealed up in clear plastic bags. How like the clichéd serial killer he'd enjoyed taking things apart to see how they work. He looked out over what remained of the sea and noticed how the clouds, like those behind the *Psycho* house, were moving in abnormal ways. He listened to the sounds of the wretched Mumbaikars below him, knowing so well their collective mien that he no longer had to look. Instead, he watched the clouds shrink and swell like vast white lungs against the blackness of the sky and waited for all the many discrete elements to reconfigure themselves inside his head.

Kaal sat in an armchair in bedroom 3,

his back to the terrace, listening to NB's head coming apart. There'd been days of it, one more would make a week, and extracting any fragments of sense had demanded its commensurate quota of teeth. Excluding a handful of times when he'd filmed nocturnal prowls in and around the Barn, talking to himself and gesturing as if to hostile presences, either blocking his way or else following him undeterred for every step of his increasingly erratic routes, he had not left the sweat and the gloom of his plastic sheet. But whether his knees were under his chin or jerking sporadically about the Barn and the surrounding roof, the thoughts that left his mouth were never less than ambulatory, never less than everywhere at once and nowhere and outside of time.

NB's head was in so many pieces that what meaning Kaal could glean from his post facto surveillance had to be pieced together over days, assiduously formed and reformed from pages and pages of hastily scribbled notes. While he'd largely given up on uncovering anything revelatory amongst the interminable *Psycho* esoterica and pseudo-mystical art theory, most of it scrambled to the point of being cryptographic, by the end of the first day, there was nevertheless the gleam of something lucid surfacing from this maunderer's swampland that could not be so easily dismissed as yet more conceptual drool. And it was not only the volume of references or the broken down timbre of the voice that intimated its possible significance, but the relevance somehow to Kaal's own predicament, enhanced by NB's transitions to the second person, that raised his skin again like cold air.

The notes he'd compiled on these utterances were something to which he assigned importance without being able to claim anything like full comprehension. He thought of them as ineluctable evidence, but exactly what they were supposed to be evidence of he had no idea. As had become his habit, he felt it in his limbs before he ever managed to accommodate it in his head.

What eventually became clear from the assembled pieces was NB's realization that the installation had assimilated him, and that he wasn't some independent augmentation of the work but rather foreseen, planned for, and consequently accommodated with no more difficulty or consternation than the audience itself. That, in short, he'd been set up. By MC, or if not by her then by someone she'd talked to that she shouldn't have. His one consolation was the thing he'd done that they couldn't have predicted, the errant consequence that would be discovered when it came time to dismantle the Barn. And yet despite the imagined shock, the succour this yielded remained slight in comparison to the abject shame he felt at having been made art of at the expense of his own project. To have become the Barn's auxiliary act... no, worse in fact, to have become completely subsumed by it was for NB an unbearable revelation, and one which went some way to explaining the increasingly garbled manner of its disclosure.

As Kaal listened and made notes, the words came to resemble his own confession, eventually undermining his isolation to the stage where the anxiety he felt crawling up the back of his neck demanded that numerous breaks be taken in order that his own head remain in one piece.

He did his best to imagine two images

side by side, to picture them in his head, which sounded feasible but never was: Marion's screaming mouth at the beginning of the shower scene, water streaming off her teeth, and beside it a salivating Xenomorph, glistening and metallic, just before it dispatches Parker in Alien.

Kaal began thinking how, in *Psycho*, when Hitchcock wants to hide something he shows it from above. How the birds-eye view does not care about who is doing what or why they are doing it, because its sole task is to perpetuate mystery through indifference. And how the apocalypse can be thought of as the inverse of this perspective, coming up from underneath, or emerging from the inside, and thus disclosing what was formerly hidden. The apocalypse, then, releases us from the suspense of life and the subterfuge of the world; it engages with the real at the expense of what was formerly taken for the real, which collapses in on itself in order to divulge the thing or state that it previously concealed.

And so it struck Kaal that this was why the murders in *195 Days…*, though ostensibly real, seemed less real than the faked events they re-enacted, why it was when the fake slayings were realized they were at the same time made less real. For the anterior reality was not thereby sacrificed but rather consolidated, made more real by the actualization of the original imitations. And that these events were each time witnessed from an elevated position only served to confirm their status as distractions, as yet more layers obscuring whatever fundament might be sequestered inside or behind it.

Both Kaal and NB had seen the knife go in, come out, and go back in again, seen the blood spurting from the bodies, seen that it was not Hershey's or Bosco's chocolate syrup, and yet, minus the jump-cuts, the angles and the score, there was just the ridiculous banality of killing, a combination they found difficult to reconcile with any of their standard versions of reality. Too unlikely and too mundane: the quintessence of life, of course, and yet that which least resembled their conception of it.

He'd been stood watching the bagged body on the terrace walk in circles long enough for his legs to start aching. He dragged a chair from the dining table and positioned it in front of the sliding glass doors and sat down. The body outside continued its slow circumferential shuffling. With so much else unexplained he'd told himself that he didn't need to know what had gone on inside the black plastic sack, that it made sense in the context of everything else that had happened, and that his failure to understand it was just a continuation of that same lack of comprehension – and further, that it was inevitable and even desirable. But that this was something it was within his power to examine directly meant that his curiosity had grown into a near-irrepressible desire to act. He watched, knowing he didn't have long left, knowing he would have to look and that any previous lack of nerve had now been supplanted by the increased closeness of the groundswell.

He got up and slid the glass door open just enough to pass through. Inside his head in an instant: the smell of decay sweetening in the sun. Standing there ankle-deep in flies, he called out to the circling body. There was the slightest of pauses before it continued on its way. He shouted out again, the pause longer this time. Passing on the left of the body, he went to the edge of the terrace and looked over: a disgusting ocean of faces, half-dissolved with hunger and abjection, looking back at him, their bodies being clawed at, eaten, from the waist down, close enough now to see without the aid of his binoculars. Everywhere he looked were hands grabbing, punching, scratching, fingers digging at eyes, going inside mouths, pulling at cheeks, not coming out again. The noise, pitchy yet uniform, arrived from everywhere at once, even the sky, even the space behind him, like the wail of a sick animal lamenting its continued sentience.

He turned and walked towards the body, not thinking, imagining nothing, took hold of the black plastic sack at the top with both hands and pulled. It came off in one barely hindered movement.

Although the decibels were undiminished and the sky clear, the once cacophonous noise seemed to abate, and the heat from the sun seemed to cool as if from a passing bank of cloud. The flies too appeared caught in this momentary lull, paused in their chaos like tiny parts of a stilled explosion. The body, which had become more than one body, in keeping with this generalized cessation, stopped and turned to face him. He backed away from it, from its additional half-formed head, superimposed yet slightly left of centre over the original, away from its extra underdeveloped arms growing out the larger arms like subsidiary branches, from the protuberances drooping from the knees, through the torn trousers, that he took to be unfinished feet.

It was as if the man in front of him, who despite his unnerving supplementations was still short of needing to be pluralized, was the physical manifestation of some midpoint in a cinematic dissolve. Like when Lila and Sam are standing out the front of the Fairvale Church and the shot dissolves into them driving to the Bates Motel, and there is momentarily the suggestion of there being two Lilas and two Sams, as they are ghosted at once by their futures and their vestigial selves. Although, in this instance, the original man was quite clearly dead, displaying signs of decomposition in his feet, hands and face, the resulting fusion's rudimentary animation coming exclusively from the later, supervening identity. The only explanation he had was that the now dead man had divided while in the process of dying, and that this confluence of corpse and part-formed living human, this mush area, was the unfortunate result.

The face that hovered over and marginally to the left of its now inanimate predecessor opened its mouth as if to speak, but no words came out. Aside from the weak, faintly bronchial pattern of the breathing, his efforts to talk produced no sound at all. Frustrated by this impotence, he kept trying, his auxiliary face contorting into scarcely human shapes in an effort to make the desired communication. As he continued, his eyes gradually widened and became increasingly glassy, glaring and desolate as they petitioned his would-be interlocutor for some small sign of recognition. But his confused silence received only the same in return, for while his host's murderer stood there doing his best to translate the lip movements into words, he wasn't able to, and the longer it went on the more he suspected that the mouth he was attempting to read was working with a completely unfamiliar vocabulary. In fact, the oddness of the various muscle arrangements led him to question whether the language trying to get out was even human.

They remained there exchanging stares, each as dazed and remote as the other, until finally the body was invited inside. It hesitated, the mouth still trying to speak, but was eventually cajoled, by a series of gesticulations and smiles, off the terrace and into the main living area of the apartment. The body was directed to the sofa, and they both sat down next to each other, a person's width between them. Despite the body's despairing attempts, neither one spoke. They sat looking out of the glass sliding doors, watching blankly as the first of the horde climbed up over the terrace wall.

Reducing speed makes the discontinuous

continuous: individual movements and gestures and facial expressions become harder to discern. The same happens when speed is increased. The difference lies in the possibilities for meaning: maximized in the one and all but eradicated in the other.

At a particular juncture in the 7th and 8th

iterations of the Central Park shower scenes, NB and Kaal saw something that they had not noticed before, something made possible by the extreme slowness of what unfolded. They saw the dying woman defending herself, her right hand splayed at arm's length in front of her, which from the angle of the Met roof, and for no more than a second, became something of such jolting singularity and conclusive arrangement that both parties were fiercely discomposed, on and off, from that point on.

What they saw was the back of Marion's head become something else, as through some fleeting harmonization of light, shadow and the disarray of wet hair, it was transformed into the clear and unmistakeable representation of a face; and around that face, extending from the head like five organic prongs were the silhouettes of her fingers, trembling, and spewing, so it seemed, thousands upon thousands of miniscule particles from their ends – projections that either side of this instant were indistinguishable from the fine raindrops of some passing summer shower.

Kaal returned to this image more often than felt sane: freeze-framing, staring, scrutinizing, second-guessing his eyes. For the problem was the face that he saw, in each instance, was his own face, and however much he looked he could not unsee it.

Lila is repeatedly shot in front of a rack

of four leaf rakes, situated at the front of Sam Loomis' hardware store, so that the tines of all four rake heads appear to obtrude from her head like some alien growth.

"Of the cars on offer at California Charlie's

used car lot, Marion studies the licence plates of three cars that she does not purchase: RWS... (Real World Scenario), ANI... (As Nature Intended), and PGM... (Path Generation Method). In doing so she rejects the most credible courses of action and opts instead for that which she feels will reflect and ultimately reinforce her thought processes, that which will offer her the mental control she lacks: NFB... (neurofeedback – care of Norman Francis Bates)." The retroactive influence of these acronyms did not appear to concern him, as if it weren't even an anomaly, as if backward causation were a given.

While the literalization of manmade famine

came with its own solution, access to water was not so easily remedied. But then it seemed as if the fission products were less dependent on it (or else the high salt content in the blood they consumed had no adverse effect), and could survive for long periods with virtually no sustenance. There was also the possibility, he seemed to remember reading somewhere, that a percentage of the population could act as siphonozooids, serving to regulate the water supply of the horde, perhaps by bleeding a more watery version of standard human blood.

As Kaal exited bedroom 3 into the hallway,

there waiting by the front door was the old man.

"How did you get in?"

"The door was open. I wondered if…"

"No. The door wasn't open."

"Then how did I get in?"

"I don't know."

"You must have left it open by mistake."

"That wouldn't happen," he said, suddenly less sure than he should have been.

"I don't have an answer then."

"What do you want?"

"The others are gone. I was checking…"

"Where? Gone where?"

"Out the window, some of them. There are the remains of the rest. They were too many in the end to stay. I had to barricade them in."

"And us?"

"It's different for us."

"Because the story's over and we're still going?"

"Yes, something like that."

"Like *Psycho*."

"Yes, I suppose so, just like *Psycho*."

"You arranged us being here didn't you: the segregation, the generators, the extra food."

"I played my part, yes."

"And those girls, what did you do with them?"

"What girls?"

"Those three young girls from Dharavi."

"Lots of girls in Dharavi."

"That you did things to?"

"Me? No. What is it you're saying?"

"The Rani daughters. You know the Rani daughters, right?"

"I heard of the family, of course."

"And this is you," Kaal said, handing him a photograph.

"No, this isn't me. This isn't anyone," he said, handing the photograph back.

Kaal looked at the photograph and saw that the old man was right: it wasn't of him or anyone else, but instead a deep curvilinear scratch cut into an inferior type of wood. "No, this wasn't... I was given a picture of you by Mrs Rani. I didn't realize at first, but it was you. This isn't..."

"You think I was touching them."

"What would you think?"

"I'd look more carefully before thinking anything."

"So you weren't."

"So nothing. So what you think you know, you don't."

"Like why I'm here?"

"Like why you're here."

Kaal's legs start to shift and lurch, becoming increasingly regulated until he was stood there walking on the spot. He grabbed at his thighs, trying to stop them, but couldn't.

195 Days… didn't so much end as fold in

on itself. By the final 195th day the screen had displayed, but for the odd wobble of illumination from outside the plastic sheet, nothing but uninterrupted blackness for more than a week. The audio had been limited to grunts, shuffling and the murmur of the diminishing crowds, until by way of a footnote to this last phase NB spoke. The voice when it came sounded altered, and only vaguely reminiscent of its usual sound, as if modified, as if imitating the noise NB's ghost might make. These were the words that arrived:

"Copies or remakes exploit sameness for the sake of difference. Their value resides in the contextualized and numerical deviation of that sameness. However, the truth is not to be found in all these subtleties of surface, in the theoretical patina, but in the inexplicable ooze, the horrific, slimy universality at their core, the singular gungy terror of being, the heterogeneous sickness of existence, the gloopy alien insides that through our mirrorings and copies and multiplications we desperately try to evade, to cover up. We say even in sameness there is difference, but when the universe replies it tells the opposite story. And this is its revenge."

And exactly one hour later he spoke again and for the last time:

"Sameness masquerading as difference, difference masquerading as sameness, and underneath these seemingly endless laminas an undifferentiated black pus, an ancient blood from an even more ancient wound, the confluent, unfiltered sludge of life, the raw effluence of being which for millennia has remained resistant to all our affectations of meaning, our fabricated humanity, so that to see or taste or touch it is to experience a horror beyond even our capability to think it, an annihilating terror, an ooze that absorbs all our feeble extrapolations and exudes nothing but its own entropic glut in return. The emptiness at the heart of all protestations of fullness, the life force of rot, the hope-eating slime of some unthinkable corruption of nothingness. What's left but finally uniting with what we've been too timorous to even acknowledge? What's left but this mutual ingestion?"

The closing images of *195 Days...* were

of NB sat cross-legged beside the northern-most barrel where, having pierced a hole in its side with the tip of his knife, he drank avidly of its contents. He remained there for the last two minutes, and was still there when the picture started to break up, shredding and flickering until there was nothing left but a grey-green rectangle and the faintest gurgling noise, as if from a swamp.

The terrace was overrun in seconds, and

it took just a few more before there was no other view through the glass than that of faces looking in. And yet despite the rapid influx of bodies, the doors, the glazing and the frames, remained intact. He watched hand after hand sliding slowly down the glass, but there was no thumping or kicking, no percussive attempts at entry whatsoever. In keeping with this sudden passivity, the faces themselves seemed strangely calm, looking in at Kaal and the malformed creature on the sofa next to him with something he was tempted to identify as reverence, or perhaps confusion – and if neither of these, then an automated acquiescence, a revised powerlessness no longer hidden on the fringes of consciousness, but instead clamped around every muscle like so many tiny white-knuckled hands.

Kaal stood up without forming the intention. The lack of deliberateness spun him out momentarily. For while he'd been experiencing these actions arising as if from nowhere intermittently since the start, he had not become any more accustomed to their disorientating effects. Their seemingly purposeless origins had evaded him the way all voids evade thought, and he'd continued in the only way he could: constructing his premeditations retroactively as a way of not disappearing. Standing there looking down at the incompletely divided man on the sofa, who again was attempting to have his mouth form words and failing, he went through the same corrective process to reinstate himself as the reason for his upright position. But it didn't stop there, and he found himself walking towards the front door of the apartment, again bereft of any advance design. Acutely giddy, he tried to stop thinking altogether, but all he had were thoughts and they would not disperse or fade or accommodate his body, which had arrived at the door, opened it and entered the hallway outside.

During the four-or-so minutes it took Kaal to reach the roof, he had not managed to own a single step. He had watched his progress, his legs' foreshortened steps from above and his upper half in various reflective surfaces along the way, as if he were the mere dream of this familiarly mysterious figure, a dream now forgotten in the midst of a new wakefulness lacking all requisites for any such extrapolations of proprietary prerogative. He arrived there on the roof as if a passenger of himself, and was losing sense every second of what this and other thoughts like it could mean; and of himself even, as being anything but some stubborn and demonstrably perverse bout of cerebral dyspepsia. So that when he saw the old man standing at the edge looking over he could hardly bring about the sounds necessary to draw his attention.

And yet, those tendrils of aphasia shrinking just as quickly to nothing, the old man's name got said, inducing him to turn. He looked younger than the last time he'd seen him, or else just happier than he'd ever seen him. He smiled and beckoned Kaal to where he was standing, and Kaal responded as directed without needing to respond. They looked over the edge and out across the now comparatively plateaued tract of degenerated humans, between them covering the 180 degrees from what was South Mumbai to Kaal's right across Mill Lands to Central Mumbai on the old man's left. The noise was diminished, the remaining hum almost euphonic, and the movement on the surface conspicuously less frenzied than usual. There was an expectation to the expanse, as if it were waiting on something, as if the world was about to end all over again and all there was to do was pause and watch.

Although Kaal hadn't noticed it, he'd been stooping since standing up from the sofa, so that when his back straightened his eyeline became raised by just over an inch. The effect was dramatic and it felt like his legs should have given way in response; but they stayed where they were, as rigid and as foreign as he'd now come to expect.

An indistinct swirl of what he'd taken to be flies was completely transformed in that moment, the otherwise trivial shift in perspective altering what Kaal had previously seen as nothing more than an amorphous spread of flying insects into the explicit depiction of something both horrifically familiar and eerily incongruous, as there hovering over the horde was a huge inverted plughole. With the exception of being capsized, it was the same in all regards: same chrome surround, same angle, same darkness at its centre. And just for a split-second there was something else there, the outer area having spread to form a more irregular margin, to form Norman's peephole, and then it was gone.

Having paid close attention to Kaal's reaction – his hands clenched tight around the guard rail, his eyes staring straight ahead as if locked that way post-mortem – the old man began slowly retreating towards the stairs.

Kaal's head gradually tipped back as he watched the plughole rise farther and farther from the horde. He watched it merge seamlessly with the cloud. At the exact moment that the faint but unmistakeable semblance of an eye appeared there at its centre, his head exploded, sending millions of infinitesimal filaments into the air and out across the muted faces of the still inert multitude.

Within seconds, the heads and upper torsos of the crowning layer had started to melt. As the faces came off there was a midpoint, a literal dissolve, in which both the facial features and the bone underneath were momentarily visible. Skin and bone bubbled and dripped and eventually collapsed into a murky liquid that on contact with surrounding bodies appeared to dissolve them and so increase its mass.

As the horde became fluid the level dropped, until ultimately the surface was perfectly flat and smooth and uniformly blackened, at which point the thick oil-like substance rose up at various locations, stopping and pooling on the undersides of the clouds, before flowing towards the aperture and being drawn up inside it like blood down a plughole.

With their bodies disintegrating it was

not possible for the people at the GMS Grande Palladium to be sure whether or not the building around which they were circled, piled at its perimeter as if on some invisible barrier, had started to rise up from the ground, or whether or not it was that same GMS they saw seconds later ascending diagonally above their profoundly softened heads. Only the old man himself could testify whether, having vacated its plot in Kalina, it paused over the World One Tower to retrieve him before disappearing up into the hole in the sky. Similarly, no one was left anywhere that was still certain it was the heads exploding above them that caused what happened next, whatever that was, it being so much more irresolvable with eyes and brains and everything else turning liquid the way it did.

There was an instance, one afternoon

sometime during the middle of his stay in the Tower, when Kaal felt like he'd made sense of what was going on, when all the stark peculiarities of his recent existence consolidated for a few seconds to form something approaching an answer. He was watching the screen and NB was there looking back at him. When Kaal had stretched to alleviate a mild ache at the base of his spine, NB had initiated the same movement less than a second later. When he'd scratched at his cheek and behind his right ear there was NB performing the exact same actions. For the time he remained there at the screen, NB was right behind him with everything he did, every gesture, every facial expression, every word said. What he did to keep himself sane was to construct a story about how he'd seen this part of the footage before and was in fact mimicking from memory what NB was about to do. He knew then that he was conceiving the story and what it was the story was doing: it was doing what it had to do to keep the world where it was and him inside it.

CPSIA information can be obtained
at www.ICGtesting.com
Printed in the USA
LVHW111413251020
669761LV00004B/930